D0250821

She throbbed with the passion he had aroused

"This shouldn't have happened," Willow whispered. "But that doesn't mean I don't—"

"If you're going to say you love Richard, don't!" Adam simply stared at her for a moment, then told her softly, "You're in love with love, Willow. Admit it."

She tried hard to control her voice. "I—I've admitted it was wrong of me to—to behave as I did just now, but it doesn't change how I feel about Richard!"

"And just how do you feel about Richard?" Adam asked quietly, ominously.

Willow was no longer sure how she felt, but Adam mustn't know. "I'm going to marry him," she insisted shakily.

"Because he's a good catch," Adam interpreted, and Willow's reaction was swift and instinctive. Her hand connected hard with his cheek.

REBECCA STRATTON
is also the author of these
Harlequin Romances

2091—INHERIT THE SUN
2106—MORE THAN A DREAM
2131—THE SIGN OF THE RAM
2141—THE VELVET GLOVE
2154—DREAM OF WINTER
2173—SPINDRIFT
2180—IMAGE OF LOVE
2201—BARGAIN FOR PARADISE
2222—THE CORSICAN BANDIT
2261—LOST HERITAGE
2268—THE EAGLE OF THE VINCELLA
2274—LARK IN AN ALIEN SKY
2303—CLOSE TO THE HEART
2339—THE TEARS OF VENUS
2356—APOLLO'S DAUGHTER
2376—TRADER'S CAY
2399—THE INHERITED BRIDE
2405—THE LEO MAN
2434—THE SILKEN CAGE
2452—THE BLACK INVADER
2466—DARK ENIGMA
2489—THE GOLDEN SPANIARD

and these
Harlequin Presents

106—YELLOW MOON
121—THE WARM WIND OF FARIK

Many of these titles are available at your local bookseller.

For a free catalog listing all titles currently available,
send your name and address to:

HARLEQUIN READER SERVICE,
1440 South Priest Drive, Tempe, AZ 85281
Canadian address: Stratford, Ontario N5A 6W2

Charade

by

REBECCA STRATTON

Harlequin Books

TORONTO • NEW YORK • LOS ANGELES • LONDON
AMSTERDAM • PARIS • SYDNEY • HAMBURG
STOCKHOLM • ATHENS • TOKYO • MILAN

Original hardcover edition published in 1982
by Mills & Boon Limited

ISBN 0-373-02508-4

Harlequin Romance first edition October 1982

Copyright © 1982 by Rebecca Stratton.
Philippine copyright 1982. Australian copyright 1982.

All rights reserved. Except for use in any review, the reproduction or utilization
of this work in whole or in part in any form by any electronic, mechanical or
other means, now known or hereafter invented, including xerography,
photocopying and recording, or in any information storage or retrieval system,
is forbidden without the permission of the publisher, Harlequin Enterprises
Limited, 225 Duncan Mill Road, Don Mills, Ontario, Canada M3B 3K9. All the
characters in this book have no existence outside the imagination of the
author and have no relation whatsoever to anyone bearing the same name
or names. They are not even distantly inspired by any individual known
or unknown to the author, and all the incidents are pure invention.

The Harlequin trademarks, consisting of the words HARLEQUIN ROMANCE
and the portrayal of a Harlequin, are trademarks of Harlequin Enterprises
Limited; the portrayal of a Harlequin is registered in the United States Patent
and Trademark Office and in the Canada Trade Marks Office.

Printed in U.S.A.

CHAPTER ONE

Willow Grahame was determined not to let the man beside her know just how anxious she was. Or that more than once during the flight from England she had had second thoughts about coming almost nine thousand miles with him to meet his family. It was too late to have second thoughts now, but Willow had never been more apprehensive about meeting anyone than she was about meeting Richard le Brun's family, no matter if he had assured her she would be very welcome.

His family, and that meant only one half-brother and an aged grandmother, would almost certainly treat her as politely as they would any guest to their home, but Willlow would have felt more confident if Richard had not so often regaled her with tales about them both. His grandmother was a complete autocrat, according to Richard, and she did not approve of him for various reasons; she was, he insisted, formidable.

Although she had left her native France as a young girl and lived for close on eighty years in Hawaii, she still considered herself to be a Frenchwoman and an aristocrat. Adam le Brun, Richard's older half-brother, had also figured largely in his anecdotes of home life, and according to him possessed all the arrogance and pride of the old le Bruns.

Having no claim to blue blood herself, Willow found the prospect of meeting the autocratic le Bruns more and more awesome as the moment got nearer. Her own family was much more down-to-earth, and meeting Richard had been like getting a glimpse of a completely different world, and from what she had seen of it so far it was every bit as exotic and exciting as it had promised to be, scenically at least.

Willow herself was bound to catch any man's eye, with her deep auburn hair and green eyes, and Richard le Brun wasn't the kind of man to let the grass grow under his feet. He had seen her first when he came into the library where she worked one day, and from then on had become a regular caller. Visits to the library to see her had led inevitably to meetings outside work, and things had quite naturally developed from there.

Her family had been utterly charmed by him, for Richard could charm the birds from the trees if he put his mind to it, and only her eldest brother had expressed any doubt about her going such a long way without being firmly engaged. Neither of her parents had seen cause for alarm, however, and as her mother had pointed out, it was only a matter of buying a ring to make it official.

There was also the fact that as well as being good-looking and charming, Richard was staggeringly wealthy, and therefore an eminently suitable fiancé for anyone. Willow had known him for about three months and the general opinion was that it was time enough, and no one took too much notice of Ash, her eldest brother's, doubts, because he had always been over-protective where Willow was concerned.

She had passed through the various controls at the airport in a kind of daze, then Richard had collected his car and drove them along a wide, dusty highway with fields of low-growing pineapples on either side. He turned his head for a second and looked at her as they sped along the highway, reaching over to press her hands where they lay tightly clasped together on her lap.

'I still can't believe you're here,' he told her, and his deep blue eyes glowed as he smiled, encouraging her to smile as well, but much less confidently.

His accent was a curious blend of American and Oxford English, and Willow was aware that his ancestry was an even more exotic mixture, as so many Hawaiians' were. His father had been French with a dash of Portuguese, and his mother a mingling of Irish, Italian and English, although Richard counted himself entirely American and he sometimes ridiculed his family's pride in their aristocratic origins. Both his parents had been killed in a car crash seven years earlier, when Richard was sixteen and he had been left in the dual charge of his Grandmother le Brun and his much older half-brother, Adam.

He squeezed her hand again as he tried to look into her face, not an easy matter while he was driving at speed along the highway. 'You're not nervous, are you Willow?'

Glancing at him from the corner of her eyes, Willow found herself being honest despite her earlier attempts to hide it. 'I'm scared stiff,' she told him. 'What do you expect, Richard, when I've been whisked halfway around the world to meet——'

'My family,' Richard cut in with a smile. 'And I wish you'd call me Rich—Richard makes me sound like Little Lord Fauntleroy!'

It was an old argument, and Willow shook her head as she always did. 'I like Richard better,' she insisted, 'and you said yourself that your family don't like to hear your name abbreviated. It wouldn't get me off to a very good start if they heard me calling you Rich when I arrived.'

'Oh, come on, darling,' Richard told her, laughing at her expression, 'nobody's going to eat you! Grand'mère won't because she believes firmly in *noblesse oblige*, and Adam is much too male to want to chase off a pretty girl like you, even though you are out of his age-group! Don't worry about Adam, his bark is a lot worse than his bite.'

But Willow did worry about him, for in telling her about his autocratic relatives Richard had made Adam le Brun sound by far the more formidable of the two. She could believe that an old lady of eighty-six could be autocratic, but she was hardly likely to be as overpowering as her elder grandson promised to be.

Adam le Brun ran the huge family business concerns since the death of their father seven years before, and he had also insisted that Richard should go to Oxford in deference to his mother's wishes. The fact that Richard had obeyed him suggested that he was indeed a formidable man, and Willow couldn't help assuming that he would view with suspicion the fact that not only had his young half-brother failed to gain even one qualification, but was landing them with a strange girl whom he expected them to accept as his fiancée.

As far as she could gather too, Richard was expected to join the family business now that he had completed his education, but Richard had ideas of his own. His own ambitions ran to a musical career, although he was rather vague as to the type of music he had in mind, and Willow suspected that one of his reasons for wanting her there was to help bolster his revolt against his brother's plans for him.

He turned once more and looked at her enquiringly, and Willow shook her head. 'You know your brother better than I do, naturally,' she allowed, 'but I find it hard to believe that he doesn't mind being stuck with your brand-new fiancée for several months.'

'Well, you'd better believe it,' Richard assured her with a confident smile. 'Haven't I told you, he's quite intrigued with the idea of me being engaged?' He laughed softly and squeezed her hand again, even though they were travelling at speed. 'Sooner or later one of us had to take the plunge, but neither of us could have guessed it would be me who got hooked first! Adam'll think I've gone weak in the head!'

It wasn't a remark guaranteed to bolster her confidence, and Willow looked at him doubtfully. 'That hardly sounds as if he'll welcome me, Richard.'

'Rich,' he corrected her automatically, then shook his head. 'Stop worrying, will you? Anybody would think I was taking you to a madhouse, the way you keep on worrying about it. Relax, will you?'

Willow did her best, but she couldn't get Adam le Brun out of her mind. 'Is he like you?' she asked after a few moments, and realised that she had no idea what he looked like; physically he was still very much an unknown quantity. 'I mean, do you look alike?'

Shaking his head, Richard laughed at his own frankness. 'Not at all, he's not nearly as good-looking as I am!'

'*I* see!'

She too was laughing at his conceit, but at the same time she felt he was probably telling the truth, for it was easy to believe that there couldn't be two men as good-looking as Richard in one family. His hair, which he wore fairly long, was light brown and his eyes were blue, a deep, dark blue that he probably owed to his Irish ancestry, and they were mostly smiling. In fact he had little to be gloomy about, except perhaps the plans he had for his future that did not coincide with his brother's. He was also quite aware of his attractions and was quite disarmingly conceited about them.

'Not that Adam is hideous, mind you,' he told her with a glint of laughter in his eyes. 'The le Brun charm hasn't bypassed him and he's had his share of *affaires*. With Adam they're always *affaires de coeur*, he's a whole lot more French than I am, which is why Grand'mère approves of him!'

Willow, who knew of Adam le Brun only as a much older brother and erstwhile co-guardian of his young half-brother, began to wonder if she hadn't got entirely the wrong idea of him. She had visualised him as almost middle-aged, probably because of Richard's habit of referring to him as 'old Adam' from time to time, and she had imagined him stern and rather straitlaced with no interest outside running the family firm. Richard's latest revelation made her realise that she would probably have to rethink her whole conception of the man, and she had no idea what to expect now.

'I hadn't thought of him in that light,' she confessed, and Richard's blue eyes quizzed her for a moment before he shook his head.

'I hope you never do,' he told her. 'You stick with me and leave Adam to the more experienced talent, like Marsha Sai-Hung.'

Looking at him curiously, Willow wondered how serious he was. 'Who,' she asked, 'is Marsha Sai-Hung? She sounds like something out of a very cheap movie.'

Apparently Richard found her assessment amusing, for he laughed aloud as he shook his head, and his eyes gleamed. 'Not a *cheap* movie, darling,' he told her. 'Marsha is a top-drawer, grade one elegible heiress, and as dangerous as a bundle of dynamite if she's crossed. Her daddy owns the next biggest piece of the action to the le Bruns, and she's had her almond eyes on old Adam ever since she got out of high school. Which,' he added with a malicious twinkle, 'was a bit before my time, I might say.'

Willow's smile was almost a grimace and she watched his good-looking profile curiously. 'Oooh, that was bitchy!'

'Maybe,' Richard acknowledged cheerfully. 'But if you think that was bitchy you ain't seen nuthin' yet. Bitches take lessons from dear Marsha, and she especially likes to take a crack at other females and younger brothers, so stay clear!'

'Is she attractive?'

'Physically, you mean?' He shrugged, and Willow suspected it was because he didn't like bestowing praise of any kind on a woman he so obviously disliked. 'She's stunning in a slinky, silky oriental way, if you know what I mean, but definitely not the sweetness and light type, except around Adam. She positively purrs around him!'

It was all very intriguing and not at all like she expected, and Willow nodded thoughtfully. 'If she's as stunning as you say and she's so friendly with your brother, why hasn't he married her?'

'Because Adam isn't the marrying sort,' Richard said, as if it was something she should have known. 'And he knows that any woman he marries will have to pass Grand'mère's eagle eye. She figures that nothing but a French wife will do for the head of the le Bruns, and

Marsha is like me in that she's a real Hawaiian mixture of races.'

'She's American, isn't she?'

'Sure she is, so's Adam, and me *and* Grand'mère, whatever she has to say about it, but that's how it stands.'

'I see, then I'm surprised that Marsha—what's-her-name—hasn't married someone else just to show him,' Willow declared. 'I know I would in her place.'

'So she did,' Richard informed her casually. 'Sai was her maiden name, she added the Hung when she married a guy called Jimmy Hung a few years back, and she thought it sounded kind of classy to have the two names, so she kept it and hyphenated them when she divorced him.'

Willow glanced at him from the corner of her eye. 'You really don't like her, do you?'

'Like a slap in the face,' Richard admitted with unabashed frankness, 'and it's mutual. I'd hate to have her in the family, and she knows it, that's why she hates the sight of me. But it's just possible that one day she'll find a way of dragging old Adam up the aisle.'

'As drastic as that?' Willow asked with a laugh, and Richard pulled a face.

'I know Adam, and brute force is the only way she'll get him there.'

Richard had described La Bonne Terre to her, but actually seeing it was an experience she would never forget. Built by the first le Brun when he arrived from France in the 1860s, the house fitted perfectly into its setting of lush gardens and magnificent trees. Hawaii was perhaps more generously endowed by nature than almost any other place on earth, and practically every type that grew there had been set in those glorious gardens. Set amid acres and acres of growing pineapples, it took Willow's breath away.

It was approached by way of a wide, dusty access road from the main highway, and even before they actually got there she got the impression of hundreds of different colours and scents. It was like driving into a dream when they drove round in front of a porticoed entrance, and as Richard braked the car to a halt he leaned back in his seat and sighed in sheer contentment.

'Home, sweet home,' he quoted, and something in his voice struck Willow as a lot less facetious than the words he used.

Whatever claims he made to be able to settle and live anywhere, and no matter what plans he had made for his future, separate and apart from his brother's, she thought he would always, in time, come back to La Bonne Terre. There was a glow in his eyes when he looked at it that she doubted any woman could inspire, and for a moment Willow felt she had been forgotten.

'It's lovely,' she said softly, and Richard turned at once and smiled at her.

'It's lovely,' he echoed, and stood for a moment after he got out of the car, gazing at the old house half buried in the rampant growth of a fragrant pink rose and golden honeysuckle. Then he turned suddenly, as if reminded he was not alone, and as he helped her from the car he laughed a little selfconsciously. 'I never realised how much I missed the old place,' he confessed.

They were already crossing a wide porch formed by an overhanging balcony, when the door opened and a big, dark-skinned woman in a brightly patterned dress beamed a smile at them. 'Richard! You bin 'spected long ago, where you bin? We think you got lost!' Her voice was throaty and she spoke with the sing-song lilt of the islands that at the moment Willow found difficult to follow. But the wide smile and cheerful face gave a brief boost to her confidence. 'Where you bin?' the woman demanded again with the familiarity of long acquaintance.

'We were held up in traffic, Luana.' He smiled and bent to plant a quick kiss on the woman's broad dark face that made her flutter her eyes like a girl. 'It's good to be home; where is everybody?'

'Mister Adam's in the *salon*,' he was informed, with a quick glance at a closed door just across the big airy hall. 'An' Madame le Brun she up in her room.'

'Sulking or getting herself dolled up?' Richard asked with a touch of defiance, and the woman shook her head reproachfully.

'You know how glad she always is to see you, *kanaka*.'

The suggestion of familiarity in the way she scolded him reminded Willow that Luana had been with the le Brun household since Richard was a small boy. She had spoiled him and spanked him, according to Richard, and he was obviously fond of her, as she was of him.

While Richard renewed an old acquaintance, Willow took the opportunity to look around. The hall was elegant but slightly old-fashioned and beautifully cool after the heat outside, thanks in part to a tiled floor and plain white walls. Paintings adorned the walls and a huge potted palm stood at the foot of a wide and elegantly curved staircase, the only furniture being a small table with a telephone on, and one or two cane chairs.

She started briefly when Richard slipped an arm around her waist and drew her close to him, and she realised that the housekeeper was looking at her with friendly but curious eyes. 'Luana,' Richard said, 'I've brought my *wahine* home to meet the family, don't you think she's beautiful? Her name's Willow—Willow Grahame—and I'm crazy about her.'

'Miss Gra-ham.' Her hand was shaken solemnly, then that wide, spectacular smile was in evidence again. 'You gon like it here, you see.' Then she turned to Richard again, urging him along with a hand on his back. 'You sure been heard come,' she told him, 'you best go in 'fore Mister Adam comes to find you.'

For a moment Richard hesitated and it seemed to Willow that he was preparing himself for the moment he would see his brother again, and it struck her as rather odd that he needed to. Nor did it do much to help her confidence. Then he pulled her into his arms suddenly and kissed her mouth firmly. 'Let's go,' he said, and led her across the hall with an arm still around her waist. Just outside the door of what had been designated the *salon* he paused again and kissed her, then turned the handle while he still looked down into her eyes, and almost collided with someone on the way out. 'Adam!'

There was no mistaking his pleasure, whatever tales he had told about his brother, and the man inside the room smiled as he stepped back to let them in. He grasped Richard's hand with both his own, and light grey eyes glowed with warmth as they looked at him. 'Welcome home, Richard!' He seemed to take in every feature of his brother's face and he was smiling still. 'It's good to see you again!'

It was his voice that most attracted Willow, for it was deep and soft and quite exceptionally beautiful in its timbre, with an accent that was entirely American but with an overtone of something else too. He had, she recalled, been educated up to university age at an island school, then gone on to university in Paris, which probably accounted for that slight overtone.

That the brothers were glad to see one another was in no doubt, and it gave Willow a curious sense of relief to realise it, for instant antagonism would have made her own position even more uncomfortable. Richard hugged her close, brushing his lips across her brow as he did. 'This is Willow,' he told his brother, and his fingers squeezed tight into her arm. 'Willow darling, this is my big brother, Adam.'

She murmured a greeting, conscious of the grey eyes taking stock of her, and when she took the proffered hand long, strong fingers closed over hers, holding them while he continued his almost too explicit study of her. 'Willow,' he echoed quietly. 'That's a most unusual name, Miss Grahame, do you mind my asking how you came by it?'

'Oh no, not at all.' Her own voice, she noticed, had an oddly breathless sound, but there was something very affecting about Adam le Brun. He wasn't a bit what she had expected, and she found that light, steady gaze very disconcerting. 'It happened because both my parents are botanists and they had the idea of giving all of us the names of trees instead of something more conventional.'

'All of you?' he queried, and seemed to suggest that there couldn't possibly be more like her, so that quite unaccountably Willow flushed.

'I have three brothers, Mr le Brun. Ash, Rowan and Larch.'

'It's a charming idea,' he remarked, although she couldn't be sure that he wasn't faintly amused too, but it was a common enough reaction for her not to take offence. Seeking her slightly evasive gaze, he held it for a moment. 'And may I call you Willow?' he enquired. 'Or should I be strictly formal and call you Miss Grahame?'

'Oh, Willow, please!'

He nodded, still watching her with that oddly disturbing gaze as they all three turned into the room. 'Did you have a good flight?' he asked, but it was Richard who answered.

'Not too bad, thanks. But we're glad to stretch our legs, eh, darling?'

Willow nodded. She wasn't exactly ill at ease, but rather excited in a way she didn't quite understand, and she realised that although she had been right to feel nervous of meeting Adam le Brun, it had been for all the wrong reasons. It was true he wasn't as conventionally good-looking as Richard, but he had a devastating kind of sexuality that his confidence and maturity made almost overwhelming, and his strongly defined features were more impressive than mere good looks.

He was exceptionally tall, something over six feet, she guessed, and he had the lean grace of an athlete, or perhaps more accurately the lithe elegance of a big cat, for there was a hint of hidden power about him that was both impressive and affecting. He wore grey slacks that were expertly tailored and obviously expensive, and a cream shirt that threw his mahogany-brown hair and deeply tanned features into sharp contrast; open at the neck, it revealed a muscular throat and a glimpse of dark flesh through its fine texture. And everything about him was much less formal than she had expected.

'I don't think I actually welcomed you to La Bonne Terre,' he remarked with a half-smile. 'Please forgive me, Willow. And I understand from Richard that congratulations are in order.' He didn't take his eyes off her even while he was addressing his brother, and Willow found them increasingly disturbing. 'I congratulate you, Richard—she isn't at all what I expected.'

In two minds whether or not to take exception to the implication, Willow eventually just smiled, because she was still feeling her way and she wasn't ready yet to cope with the kind of opposition Adam le Brun would offer. There was more than a touch of arrogance about him that she found herself resenting, but at the same time she recognised it as an integral part of his undeniable attraction.

'I presume as your brother I may kiss the bride?' he said to Richard.

She had been about to sit down, and Willow caught her breath involuntarily, while Richard frowned at him uncertainly, but nodded nevertheless. She was grasped firmly by her upper arms and turned to face him, looking directly into Adam le Brun's gleaming grey eyes for a moment before he drew her close and obliged her to tip back her head. The trouch of him was alarmingly affecting and through the softness of the silk shirt his flesh warmed her own alarmingly responsive curves, titillating her senses and making her pulse race at twice its normal rate.

'You don't mind?' he murmured, but gave her no opportunity to confirm it before he lowered his head.

His mouth was firm but gentle and it teased her lips apart with stunning and unexpected intimacy before he actually kissed her. It wasn't a particularly passionate kiss, but in some strange way suggested he was more interested in seeking her reaction than giving either of them pleasure, and Willow was reminded of those *affaires de coeur* that Richard had mentioned.

'No,' he reiterated quietly, 'you're not at all what I expected.'

Uncertain of her own feelings, Willow sought to cover her uncertainty with an air of confidence. 'I'm glad I meet with your approval, Mr le Brun,' she told him. 'I must admit I had a great many doubts about coming all this way and landing on you almost without warning; without knowing how you felt about Richard bringing me with him.'

'You didn't expect us to welcome you?' Willow didn't reply, but her expression was answer enough, and Adam le Brun was shaking his head. 'I can't think what gave you the idea we're so uncivilised as to treat a visitor, and particularly Richard's fiancée, with anything but warmth,' he said quietly. 'I guess Richard must have been exaggerating.'

'I did no such thing,' Richard denied hastily. 'I only gave Willow a rundown on what to expect when she got here, it seems only right if she was going to plunge in at the deep end! After all, you can be pretty high-falutin' at times when something doesn't just suit you.'

Adam's grey eyes held his for long enough to make Richard look away, and there was a slight flush in his cheeks too that Willow knew he must resent her seeing. 'I guess you could be right,' Adam observed coolly, then turned and gave his attention once more to Willow, indicating a chair immediately behind her. 'Please sit down, Willow, and don't take Richard's warning too much to heart. I assure you we're not nearly as uncivilised as he's probably made us out to be.'

Richard too took a chair and Willow found herself sitting between the two of them, in no doubt at all which one of them had the upper hand and firmly intended keeping it so. 'Is Grand'mère likely to be very long coming

down?' Richard asked, shifting uneasily. 'I'd like to go
and make sure that Burt doesn't scrape the paint off my
new car.'

Adam looked across at him and the faint mockery in
his eyes was unmistakable at such close quarters. 'Does
Grand'mère still put the fear of God into you?' he
asked, and Willow felt a flick of anger at the deliberate
goad.

'She scares me sick, the way she always did!' Richard
retorted with unexpected spirit. 'You know how mad
she'll be because I failed to gain a pass, Adam, and she
isn't likely to let Willow being here stop her saying so! I'd
just as soon give her time to simmer down before I see
her.'

'And what about Willow?' Adam asked quietly. 'Are
you simply going to leave her to meet Grand'mère on her
own?'

'Not on her own,' Richard insisted, obviously seeing
himself as between two stools. 'You're here, and I'm only
going to keep an eye on my car, damn it, I'll probably be
back before Grand'mère comes down.' He got to his feet
but stood fidgeting with his hands for a moment. 'Did
you tell her that I'm engaged to Willow?'

'Naturally.' Adam's coolness was in such contrast to
Richard's agitation, that she had to notice it. 'Your letters
were addressed to both of us and they've been full of little
else but Willow for the past few months, I didn't think
you were trying to keep it a secret.'

'I'm not,' Richard denied. 'How did she take it?'

'Does it matter?' Adam countered quietly, and Willow
thought she could read between the lines. Obviously their
autocratic old grandmother didn't approve of the engagement, and at the thought of that being so, her heart sank.

'You know darned well it matters!' Richard insisted in
the same complaining tone. 'Willow will very likely have
second thoughts about me if Grand'mère starts putting on
her French *grande dame* manner. You know what she's
like, and it could make things real uncomfortable for me

if she doesn't take to her, you know that as well as I do!'

'I know of no reason why Grand'mère, or anyone else, shouldn't take to Willow,' Adam told him. He turned his cool grey eyes on her for a moment, moving them slowly over her features with such explicit interest that she flushed a bright pink and her heart hammered hard at her ribs. 'No reason at all,' he said, but Richard made a short, derisive sound that was meant to be a laugh.

Except that Grand'mère isn't a man and she's not likely to be influenced the same way you are!' he retorted. 'You know how she'll play up about anyone who isn't French.'

'Then you should have thought about it and chosen a French girl!' Adam told him with a flash of impatience. He wasn't a very patient man, Willow guessed, and Richard was trying what little patience he did have. 'And for God's sake stop apologising for Willow,' he went on, 'it's neither very complimentary nor necessary!'

Unsure quite what she ought to do, Willow sat pondering on the situation. She'd seldom felt more embarrassed in her life before, and oddly enough it was Richard who embarrassed her most, for he seemed to have far less understanding of her feelings than his brother did. 'If it's going to cause too much of a problem,' she ventured in a slightly husky voice, 'I can go and stay at an hotel instead.'

'You'll do no such thing,' Adam assured her firmly. He looked up at Richard and his grey eyes gleamed with something very like derision. 'Go and put your car away,' he told him, 'I'll look after Willow for you.'

Noticing the frown that drew Richard's brows together, she almost declined the chance of being 'looked after', but clearly Richard himself was thinking along the same lines and he shook his head, his mouth tightening. 'I guess you would at that,' he remarked. 'But on second thoughts I'll wait and see Grand'mère and check on my car later!'

It was hard to believe that Adam was laughing, but he was waving an airy hand in dismissal and shaking his head. 'Oh, for crying out loud,' he declared, 'go and see to your precious car, you don't have to worry about me!'

'I'm not so sure!' Richard retorted, and again Adam's eyes gleamed with laughter.

He looked across at Willow, who sat with her hands on her lap, not at all sure that she liked being the bone of contention between them. Nor of being left alone in Adam le Brun's company when he looked at her the way he was at the moment; his eyes on her flushed face and vaguely challenging.

'You're not nervous of staying with me, are you, Willow?' he asked, and his voice was low and soft, sending little unexpected shivers along her spine. He studied her for a moment in silence, then shook his head. 'Richard knows me better than that,' he said quietly. 'I haven't yet resorted to robbing cradles.' Looking up at his brother again, he nodded dismissively. 'Go keep an eye on your car,' he told him. 'And stop acting the heavy fiancé.'

Rather surprisingly, to Willow at least, Richard made no more argument, although he did give her a long, unhappy look before shrugging his shoulders. 'I won't be very long, darling,' he told her, and there was no mistaking the tone of his voice. He was apologising. 'You'll be O.K. till I come back.'

It was pointless asking him to stay or at least to let her go with him to check on his car, for one thing because she didn't have the nerve with Adam le Brun sitting beside her, and as the door closed behind him Adam leaned forward and took a cigarette from a box on the table between them. He made no move to offer her one, but looked at her narrow-eyed through the drifting blue smoke that half concealed his face.

'I don't bite,' he promised softly, and with a faint smile that told her he knew exactly how she was feeling. 'Certainly not in these circumstances.'

Willow was still smarting from that remark about robbing cradles, and looked at him down the length of her small, straight nose. 'Mr le Brun——' she began.

'Adam,' he interrupted quietly, and held her gaze mockingly.

But Willow hesitated over the familiarity of his christian name, for she found him disturbing enough without becoming any more intimate with him so soon. 'I was wondering if I shouldn't have gone with Richard,' she ventured, and he raised one dark brow.

'I don't see why,' he told her, then glanced over his shoulder in the direction of the door. 'Anyway, my grandmother is coming and she won't take it kindly if both Richard and you run out on her.' He gave her a wry half-smile as he ground out his cigarette into an ashtray, and leaned towards her with his elbows on his knees. 'She's very old and very old-fashioned, Willow; maybe a little too autocratic for some tastes, but she's a wonderful old lady and we love her. Despite what Richard says, he's as fond of her as I am, only he puts on that front. One thing,' he added as the unmistakable tap-tap of a walking-cane was heard coming across the hall tiles. 'Grand'mère is as French now as the day she left France eighty years ago, and she prefers to be called Madame le Brun rather than Mrs.'

'I'll try and remember,' Willow promised, but her heart was beating twice its normal rate when the door opened.

Adam got to his feet in a swift, easy movement that again put Willow in mind of a large and dangerous cat. 'Ah, Grand'mère!' he said, and went forward to meet her, slipping a hand just under her arm without actually supporting her. Madame le Brun, Willow guessed, would be much too independent to accept that she needed support.

She looked incredibly old at first glance, with a small wrinkled face and sharp dark eyes, and when she saw her Willow quite automatically got to her feet, smoothing down her dress in an unconsciously nervous gesture. The old lady looked every bit as formidable as Richard had claimed, despite her eighty-six years, but there was also an unexpected air of warmth about her that Richard had not mentioned, and Willow believed that her nervousness had been noted and sympathised with.

'Adam!'

She prompted her grandson sharply, and Adam rose to the occasion, completely ignoring the sharpness of the command and smiling as he reached for Willow's hand. He folded her fingers lightly in his and gave her a small, speculative glance before drawing her closer to the old lady who now occupied the chair he had formerly occupied.

'Grand'mère,' he said in his quiet and beautiful voice, 'this is Willow Grahame, Richard's fiancée. Willow, my grandmother, Madame le Brun.'

Somehow he managed to give the title a flourish and it was obvious that the old lady both expected and enjoyed it, and the sharp eyes fixed themselves on Willow with an intensity reminiscent of her grandson's. A small and rather bony hand was extended in such a way that it suggested a royal gesture, so that Willow wondered for a moment whether she was expected to kiss it or shake it in the normal way. She settled eventually for just touching the gnarled fingers lightly, remembering, as she smiled, to do as Adam had said.

'How do you do, Madame le Brun?'

The dark eyes warmed a little. 'You're welcome to La Bonne Terre, Miss Grahame. You're English, I believe?'

Somehow she managed to make it sound vaguely like an accusation, but she was not as antagonistic as Willow had been led to believe she would be. Nevertheless her independent spirit rebelled against any suggestion that her nationality made her in any way an undesirable, and her chin was angled as she replied, 'That's right, Madame le Brun.'

'And proud of it too, I see!'

The small dark eyes gleamed, and Willow believed it was with approval. Evidently she was not averse to being challenged, and Willow saw it as one possible reason why Adam le Brun was in so much more favour with her than Richard was. 'I've never had reason to be other than proud of it, *madame*,' she told her and, although the expression did not relax, something in her manner did, and the old lady nodded.

Her accent was more thoroughly American than Willow had expected in the circumstances, although it too, like Adam's, had a faintly different overtone. 'You've plenty of spunk,' she approved with a nod. 'Not the sort I'd have seen Richard taking to. And you've red hair, which probably means you go off like a firecracker if you're crossed.'

'Not every time, *madame*,' Willow denied, rather surprised to find herself more stimulated than overawed by the old lady's manner. 'I'm normally pretty even-tempered unless I'm pushed too far.'

'And you're engaged to marry my grandson.'

'That's right, Madame le Brun.'

'Hmm.' Once more she was subjected to the scrutiny of those small but incredibly sharp eyes. 'I suppose you don't have any French blood?'

Willow had expected the question sooner or later, but she had never seen herself having enough nerve to take up the challenge as she did.

'Actually it's just possible,' she told the old lady. 'My middle brother, Rowan, takes a great interest in things like family histories, and he says there are good grounds for believing that an ancestor of ours came over from Normandy with William the Conqueror.'

'That's a claim a good many English families make, so I've heard,' Madame le Brun observed dryly. 'Still, I guess it's as likely as all the claims to descent from the Mayflower immigrants made by a lot of Americans. We all like a little history in our backgrounds.' Once more the shrewd eyes studied her intently. 'Whatever your ancestry, you're a very pretty young woman, Miss Grahame, and that makes up for a good deal. I assume that red hair is natural?'

Slightly flushed, Willow again angled her chin. 'As the good Lord made it, *madame*!'

There was a glint of amusement in Adam le Brun's eyes, she noticed as he leaned on the back of his grand-mother's chair, and the old lady was very obviously en-joying it. 'Now,' she said turning to address him once more, 'where's that other grandson of mine?'

Willow looked instinctively to Adam to answer, and he smiled across at her as he did so, obviously letting her know that he knew how reluctant she was to let on that Richard had more or less ducked out of the initial meet-ing. 'He went to see that Burt didn't scratch the paint on his new car,' Adam said. 'He won't be long, Grand'mère.'

'I think I can hear him.' Willow heaved an inward sigh of relief as she sat back in her chair again, and she listened to Richard coming across the hall.

'Grand'mère!' He came into the room and hurried across to the old lady, kissing her on both cheeks while he bent almost double to bring himself to her level. 'How are you?'

'I'm fine.' The old lady held him at arm's length for a moment, and quizzed him shrewdly. 'You've grown even more like your mother,' she informed him, and the tone of her voice made it obvious that she didn't intend it as a compliment. 'You're too handsome for your own good, and for the peace of mind of all the silly girls who run after you.'

It was the first time Willow had seen Richard com-pletely abashed, and she wondered how he was going to react. He flushed, but he had enough panache, even so, to smile down at Willow and reach for one of her hands. 'Only one girl,' he said, 'and she isn't silly, she's beautiful and smart.'

'She's beautiful and she has spirit,' his grandmother told him. 'I can't say how smart she is until I know if you've changed.'

'I have—a little,' Richard told her cautiously, and his hand clasped Willow's tightly.

'Yet you come home without a single pass to your

name,' Madame le Brun reminded him relentlessly. 'I don't call that very smart, Richard; I call it a waste of good time and money. However——' she shrugged and spread her hands in a very French-style gesture, 'I guess this isn't the time or the place to talk about it. At least you had sense enough to pick yourself a girl with spirit and some culture, now when are you going to marry her?'

Rather to her surprise, Richard looked uneasy and he didn't reply at once as she expected him to. Which was why she took it upon herself to supply an answer. 'Nothing has really been settled yet, Madame le Brun, and there's really no special hurry.'

'Hmm.' Small, sharp eyes darted from one grandson to the other, and after a moment or two she shrugged her thin shoulders in an elegant and very French shrug. 'I don't know about that, young lady.'

'We're quite happy as we are,' said Richard, finding his voice at last. 'We aren't in any desperate hurry to tie the knot, are we, darling?'

Not quite sure what to say, Willow murmured something inaudible, but it was rather disconcerting to hear Adam le Brun laugh quietly and she was aware of those cool grey eyes on her again. The next few weeks, she felt, were likely to prove much more eventful than she had anticipated.

CHAPTER TWO

'I CAN see how she would have overawed you when you were a little boy,' Willow allowed, referring to the effect Richard's grandmother had on him. 'I quite like her, but she *is* rather overpowering.'

'She's always scared me silly ever since I was a kid,' Richard confessed gloomily. They were walking in the gardens after lunch, a day or two after their arrival on the island, and it seemed inevitable somehow that Madame le Brun should be the subject of their conversation. 'She's always been here,' he went on. 'She came here when she married Grandpère and she was here when Pop married his first wife, Adam's mother, and moved in with her. Now they're all dead, Pop, Mom and Adam's mother, but Grand'mère goes on for ever.'

'She's very old, isn't she?' Willow said, and Richard nodded.

'Eighty-six; but knowing Grand'mère she'll make the hundred. Not,' he added hastily, 'that I don't want her to make it, but it's the kind of stamina she has, and she never gives in. I remember when I was in second grade at school, taking history, I always imagined Grand'mère during the French Revolution sitting and knitting like fury under the guillotine while heads rolled. Except that she'd have more likely lost her own head, of course; there's nothing of the proletariat about Grand'mère!'

'Oh, she'd certainly have been an aristocrat,' Willow agreed, and couldn't help being amused by his opinion of his grandmother.

'She was,' Richard said. 'We're none of us allowed to forget that the *famille* Chardin was very top-drawer, especially me.'

'Why especially you?' Willow asked. That curious defensiveness of his always intrigued her, and she had often wondered what the reason for it was.

The difference in Madame le Brun's manner when she addressed each of her grandsons was little enough, but it was there, and Willow had more than once suspected that it had something to do with Richard's mother; something that he seemed about to confirm. He held her hand tightly, and it was clear that whatever he was going to say needed to be thought about first.

'Mom wasn't exactly Grand'mère's ideal choice for a le Brun wife,' he told her eventually. 'In fact she was working on the production line in the le Brun canning factory when she caught Pop's eye. She was pretty, beautiful in fact, with big blue eyes and thick wavy blonde hair, and I guess Pop was man enough to need a woman. Jeanne, Adam's mother, had been dead about a couple of years and I guess he was lonely too. Anyway, when he knew I was on the way he did the right thing by Mom and they were married, but Grand'mère never really forgave him for it.'

'But why on earth not, if they were happy together?' Willow asked, although she could imagine the blow it must have been to the old lady's pride when her son married one of his less exalted employees.

'Oh, they were happy enough,' Richard mused, 'which probably made Grand'mère more mad than ever. Then, seven years ago, they were driving up to Diamond Head for a party and got into collision with a truck. They were both killed instantly.'

'It must have been a terrible shock for you.'

Willow squeezed his hand in sympathy, and he looked down at her for a moment before pulling himself back to normality. 'Yeah, well——' He smiled ruefully. 'I was sixteen at the time and I took it pretty hard, but it hit Adam hard too; he was very fond of Mom. I guess if it hadn't been for Adam I'd have gone wild with no one to keep a firm hand on me when Pop was gone. He took me over and put the brakes on me; being all that much older than me he could pull rank on me, and he did—for my own good. Mom always boasted that way back one of her ancestors had gone to Oxford and she got Pop to promise I should go if I could make the grade. Adam put me to work earning my place, and I guess it was the best thing he ever did for me.'

'So he isn't *all* bad?'

She was teasing, but Richard's expression suggested he was taking it seriously. 'Adam? He isn't bad at all, just too—arrogant at times. A real le Brun, in fact.'

Puzzled by his reasoning, Willow eyed him curiously. 'Well, so are you, aren't you?'

'Not in the same way,' Richard denied, and there was

a trace of something in his voice that suggested he regretted it, however defiant he might be. 'Adam's mother was as carefully selected as a brood mare, for her breeding and her looks. She was wholly French, which was an essential point in Grand'mère's opinion, and she came from a good family—the perfect le Brun wife. Her crowning achievement was when she presented Pop with the necessary son less than a year afterwards.'

'Adam?'

Richard shook his head. 'Jean. He was a couple of years older than Adam and he died when he was about seventeen. I was only four at the time, but I can remember how hard Grand'mère took it, and from then on she treated Adam as if he was the most precious thing in the whole world.'

The bitterness he felt just wasn't possible to disguise, and it was somehow touching. For Willow felt he wanted his grandmother's affection more than anything, even though he professed to be in awe of her. 'You sound as if you dislike her,' she suggested softly, 'and I know you don't.'

The sudden grin he gave her was more like the Richard she knew, and he tucked her arm through his as they walked. 'I love the old lady,' he told her with disarming frankness, 'but she does have the ability to scare the wits out of me, and she could ruin the impression I wanted you to have. I wanted you to feel you liked the family and the old house.'

'And so I do,' Willow assured him. 'You love La Bonne Terre, don't you?' she went on, knowing it was true, however he answered.

'I guess I always have,' Richard admitted eventually. 'But that doesn't mean I won't up and off when the time is right.'

'But won't you miss it?'

'Sure I will,' he said, 'but it's just one of those things. It'll still be my home if I ever want to come back to it. I just wish you could have seen it without Grand'mère hovering around and making you anxious.'

'I'm not anxious.' He looked at her doubtfully, and she smiled. 'I like the house and I like your *grand'mère*; you mustn't let her intimidate you.'

Richard pursed his lower lip slightly, drawing her close with an arm about her shoulders and resting his face on her hair for a moment. 'You sound like Adam,' he accused, and Willow took him up on it at once, shaking her head in quick denial.

'Oh, I'm quite sure I don't!'

They emerged from the narrow and slightly overgrown path as she spoke, and came on to the broad open area in front of the house, and Richard was looking thoughtful. 'Saying it like that you sound as if you don't much like him,' he told her. 'But I guess old Adam does keep up the French aristo bit, and he can be a real hard man when he wants his own way, but he's O.K.'

'Oh, but of course he is,' Willow hastened to assure him. 'I'm just a bit nervous of him, that's all. As you say, he's a bit overpowering, and you know how it is meeting new people.'

'Meeting new people never bothered you before,' Richard observed, and frowned at her curiously. 'Why Adam?'

'Oh, I don't know.' She laughed and shrugged, lifting the arm he had about her shoulders, and wishing they need not discuss Adam le Brun at quite such length. 'It's just that he's——' She bit her lip and hastily shook her head, laughing off the rest of the sentence, for it would never do to let Richard know that she found his brother not only autocratic, but disturbingly attractive as well.

Willow was, in fact, beginning to wish she hadn't committed herself to spending the whole summer at La Bonne Terre, for there were certain elements she found disturbing. She had expected the exotic colour and the sunshine, but it was the human element that she found hardest to cope with, and Adam le Brun was chief among those who made her uneasy.

She recalled that she had refused Richard's invitation initially, but then they had drifted into a tentative kind of engagement, and there seemed no longer any reasonable grounds for her refusing. It was all a little vague, and she had no ring as yet, but Richard liked to refer to it as an understanding, whatever that might mean.

It was a little over a week after their arrival, when they were all at dinner one evening, that Adam raised the matter of Richard joining the le Brun Corporation. It promised to be a touchy subject in the circumstances, but instead of passing it over with some noncommittal reply as Willow hoped he would, Richard stated quite categorically that he had no intention of joining the firm at all, in any capacity.

Adam looked up at once and stared at him, but it was Madame le Brun who voiced her surprise first, and her remarkably strong voice was resonant with indignation. 'What are you saying, boy?' she demanded. 'That you don't *want* to join the le Brun Corporation?'

'I guess that about sums it up, Grand'mère.' Richard kept his eyes downcast and Willow could guess how he had screwed himself up to this moment.

'Well!'

The old lady's opinion was clear enough, but Adam in his place at the top of the table said nothing for a moment. Instead he looked at Richard steadily, with the fingers of one hand curved about the slender stem of his wine glass, and his dark features strangely unfathomable. 'I assume you've given it a lot of thought,' he said quietly, and to Willow's discomfort his grey eyes flicked briefly in her direction, suggesting that he knew exactly where to place the blame for this unexpected turn of events.

'Yes, I have,' said Richard. 'I've given it a whole lot of thought.'

Adam raised his glass and took several long, slow sips of wine, while Willow sat and marvelled at his self-control. It must have been quite a blow to him to have his well-laid plans so abruptly shattered, but he made no angry accusations, nor did he lose his temper. 'I can also assume you have something else in mind, I guess,' he suggested quietly, and once more those slightly narrowed eyes were directed at Willow.

Richard too glanced briefly at her before he replied, and she didn't fail to notice the brief, quick flick of his tongue across his lips. 'I'm going to do something I'm good at,' he said.

'Oh?'

It was all too much like cat and mouse, and Willow stirred uneasily, aware that Adam had the upper hand however it looked at the moment. 'I want to be a musician,' Richard announced, and put as he put it it sounded rather naïvely schoolboyish, so that Willow wasn't altogether surprised to see Adam's wide mouth twitch briefly into a smile.

'Oh, you do?' he said. 'And what, or who, put that idea into your head?'

His meaning was in such little doubt that Willow would have objected if Richard hadn't got in first. Thrusting out his chin, he glowered defiantly across the table at his brother. 'You can cut out the hints,' he told him. 'The idea was mine, I wasn't influenced by anybody.'

'Ah-hah!' If only, Willow thought, he wouldn't watch her with those cool, knowing eyes. 'And what's Willow supposed to do while you're gadding around strumming your guitar?' Adam asked softly. 'Follow you around like a groupie?'

Willow flushed, furious on her own behalf as well as Richard's. 'That's quite uncalled for,' she protested. 'You don't even know what kind of music Richard has in mind!'

'Do you?' Adam countered swiftly, and she was obliged to shake her head. All Richard had confided in her was that he wanted a career in music, and with her own tastes in mind, she had assumed he meant a concert career.

'We've never discussed it,' she was forced to admit, and Adam's appeal with upraised eyes made her go on, rashly uncaring if she offended. 'I only knew about Richard's plans just before we took off,' she told him defensively, 'and there was too much else to occupy me to ask questions.'

'You're committed to marry a man and you don't even know what his taste in music is?' Adam asked, and the slight curl of his lip brought a flush to her cheeks.

'It was never important,' she insisted. 'We mostly went to plays when we went to the theatre, not concerts.'

Adam fixed her with that steady and infinitely disturbing gaze, and something told her that she should have known better than to tackle him; Richard was a subject he knew far more about than she did. 'Maybe,' he observed after a second or two, 'Richard is smarter than I figured. If you aren't a pop fan he might have thought you'd drift away from him, and naturally he didn't want that to happen.'

'I wouldn't have!'

'If you say so,' Adam allowed in that devastatingly quiet voice of his. 'When he left home he was crazy about playing in a group, but we hoped he'd grown out of it and had other things to keep his mind on. It seems we were wrong, which is a pity, because guitar players are a dime a dozen; more in the islands. Are you prepared to live like a beach-bum and go hungry in the hope that one day he'll make it to the top?'

'Now just a minute!' Richard protested before Willow could make her own objection. 'Nobody goes hungry— why should they?'

'As long as you're not expecting the le Brun Corporation to finance your artistic yearnings,' Adam told him, brutally frank. 'The company is exactly that—a company, and you can't expect the privileges without doing some of the work.'

It was obvious to Willow that Richard was already regretting having announced his intentions so rashly and wishing he had left it to a more opportune moment, but it was too late now, and Adam would be relentless in his opposition, she guessed. Knowing Richard as she did, she could imagine that his compliance was only a matter of time.

'I have my own money from Pop,' Richard declared. He sounded pettish and he was using his hands a great deal more than he usually did. 'I don't *need* the company's money!'

Adam laughed shortly. He had the whip hand and, to Willow's prejudiced eye, he was enjoying it. 'Your inheritance from Dad comes from the same source as everything else,' he told Richard bluntly. 'It isn't manna from heaven, it's profits that have to be worked for!'

Richard was frowning, and it was very obvious he regretted having started the controversy. Putting down his fork, he eyed his brother defiantly. 'Then I don't want the damned money!' he declared angrily. 'I'll get by without it!'

'And Willow?' Adam prompted, deceptively soft-voiced.

Willow felt the colour in her cheeks again as she came once more under the scrutiny of those grey eyes, but she refused to look up and meet them. 'Willow understands the way I feel,' Richard told him.

'If you think so.' Adam still sounded infuriatingly quiet and calm. 'But is she prepared to live the way she'll have to with only your earnings as a guitar player to depend on? That is if you can find a group willing to take you on, or a club that needs a bar-strummer. Or maybe you're thinking of putting Willow to work to keep the two of you?'

'Oh, for God's sake!' Richard declared exasperatedly. 'I'm not broke! Even without the le Brun money, I'll get by.'

'I notice you say *I'll* get by,' Adam pointed out, and Richard shook his head.

'It's my affair, damn it,' he declared. 'Leave it!'

To Willow's surprise, Adam did just that. He shrugged his shoulders then once more gave his attention to his meal, while Richard sat for a moment looking rather at a loss. The atmosphere when he eventually resumed his meal was brittle with anticipation, but not another word was said during the rest of the meal, although Willow was aware of Adam's gaze occasionally shifting in her direction, and it made her distinctly uneasy.

She found Madame le Brun's virtual silence during the exchange rather surprising too, then decided that the old

lady would be well aware that her elder grandson was
perfectly capable of handling the situation alone. She had,
however, noticed a certain gleam in the old lady's eyes
that seemed to suggest she did not despise her younger
grandson quite as much as Richard claimed she did.

When the meal was over at last and they were leaving
the table, Madame le Brun first exchanged a few words
with Adam, and then called Richard over to her, asking
him to walk with her in the garden for a while. It wasn't
a request that was easy to refuse, but although he did his
best to disguise it, Richard would far rather have gone
with Willow with the same purpose. He looked at her
helplessly when the old lady took his arm, and to Willow
the manoeuvre was so obvious that she glanced at Adam
uneasily.

'Your girl is in safe hands,' Madame le Brun remarked
dryly as she led her reluctant escort out into the garden,
and Adam's slow smile confirmed Willow's suspicions and
sent little trickles of sensation all along her spine.

Adam used one hand to indicate that she should sit
down again, but she shook her head, hovering in the open
French window as if on the point of flight. 'I think
I'd like to walk for a bit too,' she told him. 'After that
meal——'

'Stay.' Softly spoken as it was, it was nevertheless a
word of command, and to add force to it a hand was laid
lightly on her bare arm. His eyes held hers when she
looked up, startled by the move, and they were relentless
as the hand that turned her slowly to face him. 'I shan't
eat you,' he told her with a hint of mockery in his eyes. 'I
just want to talk to you.'

Willow gave him a brief, anxious glance and tried, just
briefly, to ease his hand from her arm. 'I'm not sure I
want to talk to you,' she told him, and he smiled.

'You disappoint me,' he said softly.

Taking another swift and surreptitious look at him,
Willow fervently wished she did not find him so dangerously attractive. It wasn't as if he was good-looking, as

Richard was, but Richard's kind of attraction was more obvious and much easier to cope with. Adam's more mature appeal was more potent; a virile sexuality that was much more difficult to resist, and he knew just how to make the most of it.

He wore a light suit with a pale blue shirt that gave an even icier coolness to his grey eyes, but their coolness was countered by a suggestion of hidden power, and there was a disturbingly primitive grace about all his movements. He was more dangerous than any man she had met before, and her senses responded to him in a way that alarmed her.

Nevertheless she put a bold face on it and looked directly at him, found it too disturbing and swiftly looked away again. 'I think I can guess what you want to talk about,' she told him in a slightly husky voice, 'and I don't feel inclined to discuss Richard's affairs without his being here. You very pointedly got rid of him, you and Madame le Brun; you—you ganged up on him!'

Adam was smiling slightly, his eyes mocking both her naïve opinion and her defiance. 'And you spotted it. Well, I won't deny we manoeuvred things our way——'

'*Your* way!' Willow retorted, and he shrugged.

'O.K.—my way. I have something to say to you that I couldn't say with Richard hanging around; if he'd seen through it he'd have made a fuss.'

'As he has every right to do,' Willow declared. 'I can guess that you want to talk about him taking up a musical career instead of coming into the firm, but I don't like the idea of you doing it behind his back!'

Adam's rather full lower lip pursed slightly and he looked down at her steadily, that restraining hand still on her arm. 'That sounds rather naïve,' he told her, 'but I guess you are a little naïve, aren't you, Willow?'

'Think what you like,' Willow told him, wishing she could hide the flush in her cheeks. 'I won't talk about Richard or his plans unless he's here to know what's being said. What he chooses to do is his affair, it has nothing to do with me.'

'I rather thought it did,' Adam murmured, and she instinctively shook her head.

They were standing only just inside the open French window, and the light wind that stirred the hair on her neck also carried with it the mingled scents of the garden; and in particular the perfume of the pink roses and honeysuckle that climbed over almost the whole house. It was an exotic and beautiful setting, and not one that should be marred by disagreements and family quarrels, so that Willow found herself regretting the need to fight this ruthless, strong-willed brother of Richard's.

The hand that had rested on her arm now slid around to the soft, cool skin of her upper arm and the slow movement of his thumb had a sensual, shiver-inducing touch as it moved back and forth. Looking down at her, his grey eyes held hers steadily for several moments, and a half-smile touched his lips briefly.

'Did you put him up to it?' he asked, and Willow turned on him swiftly.

'No, I didn't!'

'I wondered, that's all.'

He released his hold on her to take a cigarette case from his jacket pocket, and she noticed, as she had done once before, that he didn't offer it to her. A haze of blue smoke briefly concealed his face, but she was aware of those light eyes still watching her, and a sudden and inexplicable shiver slipped along her back. He could cause such havoc with his eyes, and she felt her femininity respond alarmingly.

'But of course you don't want him to give up le Brun's, do you, Willow?'

She looked up at him for a moment, uncertain of his meaning, but then it occurred to her that there could only be one interpretation, and a flush coloured her cheeks and there was green fire in her eyes. 'You know nothing about what I feel,' she told him, and taking a step back she glared at him furiously. 'I'm not a gold-digger, Mr le

Brun, and it makes no difference to me what Richard does for his living as long as he's happy doing it! Which I suspect is more than can be said for *you*!'

'I want to put Richard into the place his father made for him,' Adam insisted quietly, and so far he showed no sign of resenting her reckless accusation. 'He's a le Brun, whatever objections he makes to being counted one of us, and his place is in the company.'

'His place is wherever he's happiest,' Willow insisted, and took note of the only outward sign of his anger when Adam used his long fingers to ruthlessly grind the life out of his cigarette.

Turning back to her, he caught and held her reluctant gaze, placing one hand on the window frame beside her head, and he was much too close for comfort. The lean, hard body emanated a heat that touched her like fire, and she was alarmingly aware of the masculine scent that made her senses reel. That suggestion of hidden power made her think of a great cat poised to pounce, so that she caught her breath when he leaned closer suddenly, and the hard edge of his jacket touched her breast.

'Richard wants to have his cake and eat it,' he said 'He knows he can't keep himself, let alone a pretty and expensive young wife, on what he could earn playing a guitar, but it doesn't suit me to wait until he's ready to admit it. I want him in the company now, and I want you to make sure he comes in.'

'*You* want!' The reason for his wanting to talk to her alone was clear at last, and she stared at him in dazed disbelief. 'Do you seriously expect me to try and talk Richard out of doing what he wants to do, just to suit *your* plans?'

Adam smiled slowly, and little flutters of ice trickled along her spine again. 'Yours too,' he insisted. 'You're much too beautiful to trail around going hungry while Richard strums in some sleazy club, and I'm quite sure you don't really want to.'

'It won't come to that,' Willow denied, though she was

very much afraid it might, eventually, if Richard insisted on following his chosen career. 'Richard has money of his own and he can do as he likes with it.'

'As long as it lasts,' Adam agreed, but that disturbing half-smile was still hovering about his mouth. His gaze moved over her, very slowly, from head to foot, and lingered very pointedly where the neck of her dress skimmed the curve of her breasts, and again where the bodice fitted close. 'What happens when the money runs out, Willow? No money, no girl?'

'That's the second time you've made a suggestion like that!' Willow flared indignantly. 'And you don't know me well enough to make snap judgments, Mr le Brun! For your information, I mean to stand by Richard even if he hasn't a penny to his name!'

'Till death us do part?' Adam taunted in his quietly beautiful voice, and Willow's eyes flashed defiance.

'Very likely!'

'Red hair,' Adam observed coolly, looking at her slightly dishevelled head. 'Grand'mère said you'd go up like a Fourth of July rocket one of these days.'

'Now you can tell her she was right!' Willow declared, and glared at him angrily.

For a moment he said nothing, but he was close enough for her to see a fine tracery of lines at the corners of his eyes, a sketched-in web of lighter skin on the dark tan of his face that fascinated her. He was looking at her steadily and something in those cool, grey, heavy-lidded eyes suggested the kind of things she would rather not have recognised. On first acquaintance he had declared himself above cradle-snatching, but whatever his opinion of her comparative youth, Adam le Brun was making it plain that he was not above desiring his brother's girl-friend, and Willow felt strangely weak as she hastily averted her eyes.

'So,' he said softly, 'you won't co-operate?'

She was trembling and her senses responded with alarming urgency to the sheer masculine virility of him. 'I won't try and talk Richard out of something he's set his heart on,' she insisted in a breathlessly small voice.

He reached out, almost without her noticing, and placed a hand on the curve of her waist, his long fingers pressing into her flesh through the thinness of her dress, and the warmth of his palm seemed to burn into her. 'If he was half the man I'd thought him he'd have his heart set on something much different,' he said, and his voice deepened and thickened as he spoke.

The strong fingers curled more firmly, seeking to persuade her closer and, because her legs felt so curiously weak, she was unable to resist. 'Mr le Brun——'

'Adam!' He breathed his own name deep in his throat and drew her closer.

With the utmost difficulty Willow grasped at her slipping senses, and tried to bring herself back to reality. 'I—I haven't the right to try and change his mind,' she breathed huskily, but Adam was shaking his head slowly.

'Of course you have! You must have some say in your combined futures, surely?'

'Well—perhaps.' Having regained at least a little of her senses, she struggled to stay in control, but the nearness of that lean, tempting body and the long hand at her waist trying still to persuade her nearer was rapidly overwhelming common sense. 'But if—if Richard wants to play guitar,' she went on desperately, 'I haven't the right to stop him, no one has. He should have a chance to prove what he can do, even you must allow that.'

'For heaven's sake I'm not trying to sabotage his plans for the sheer hell of it!' Adam said with sudden harshness. 'You must realise that.'

'No, I don't! It seems to me you're just bent on getting your own way and you don't really care what Richard wants!'

Willow saw the way his mouth hardened, and the hand at her waist gripped her almost painfully hard. Adam le Brun, she thought dazedly, would be formidable if he lost his temper, and he looked close to it now; but his self-control was, if anything, more incredible than his determination to get his own way.

'Willow.' His voice was purring again, and she caught her breath. 'I just wish you'd try and see this from my point of view. Won't you try? Won't you help me bring Richard to his senses—please?'

It took Willow a moment or two to realise that she was being quite blatantly seduced into doing what he wanted by that almost hypnotically beautiful voice, and she shook her head back and forth in sudden and urgent denial of its influence. 'No! No, no, no! I *won't* make Richard do what he doesn't want to do!'

The gleam in Adam's grey eyes at once admired her determination and condemned her lack of co-operation, and he was shaking his head. 'Then you'll both be sorry,' he said.

'I—I don't think so.'

He stood with his hand still resting on her waist and looked at her, and every nerve in her body responded to that look. Her hands were tightly clenched into fists at her sides, and her heart was beating so violently hard that her head spun with it, and when she tried to meet his eyes she found she couldn't and looked away again quickly. 'I wish you wouldn't fight me on this, Willow,' he said, so softly that she only just caught what he said above the clamour of her heartbeat, and it jolted wildly when he placed his other hand on her waist too, and drew her closer to him.

The warm vigour of his body touched her only lightly at first, but then he put both hands in the small of her back and pressed her forcibly closer until she could feel every muscle, sense the tension in him and see the gleam of desire that changed the light grey eyes to stormy dark. 'You'll be sorry,' he promised in a harsh whisper, and lowered his head swiftly.

Willow had time only to catch a deep, startled breath before his mouth took hers with an almost savage harshness, forcing her lips apart, and demanding a response she could not resist making. His arms held her with fierce tightness, then one big hand moved upward to cradle her head in its long fingers, and imprisoned her against the demands of his mouth.

'No!'

She whispered the denial almost in panic the moment he allowed her to draw breath, and she pushed with both hands against the resisting breadth of his chest, trying to be free, but held as firmly as ever. It wasn't because the force of his assault had hurt her physically, but because of the violence of her own response that she felt so alarmed. Adam le Brun was dangerous, she had recognised it within minutes of meeting him for the first time. But getting so intimately close to the animal virility of his body had undermined her resistance more thoroughly even than she had dreamed it could, and she must make sure it didn't happen again.

It was several seconds before she gathered her chaotic senses together sufficiently to push away from him in real earnest, and her green eyes were downcast and evasive. Then she wriggled free of his arms and turned swiftly, walking out into the garden on legs that felt barely capable of supporting her. Whether or not she was going in search of Richard, she had no real idea, for her emotions were in chaos and she wasn't thinking very clearly. One thing she felt oddly sure of as she turned along a winding path through the scented shrubbery, was that however firmly she had said no to persuading Richard, Adam le Brun had somehow got the upper hand.

Even after more than a week in Hawaii, Willow was still dazzled and enchanted by the gardens of La Bonne Terre. Amid the strictly commercial acres of pineapples that had made them rich, the le Bruns had created themselves a veritable paradise that grew all the richness and variety of plants that nature was so lavish with in the islands.

Richard, she suspected, would not have walked in the gardens after lunch if she had not specifically asked him

to, for he almost always chose to drive them out somewhere. Today, however, she felt like strolling among the
wonderful colours and scents on their own doorstep, and
there were surely few places more conducive to romance,
surrounded as they were by all the richness of roses, hibi-
scus, melia and ginger as well as a hundred other species,
crowding in on all sides.

Pulling the head off one of the huge vines that climbed
up through the trees, Richard turned to face her and
tucked it behind her left ear. The huge yellow bloom
looked almost garish in contrast with her red hair, but he
seemed well pleased with the effect and nodded his satisfaction. 'There,' he said with a smile, 'that means you're
spoken for.'

'It does?' She felt a little selfconscious about it and
Willow fingered the flower head as she pushed it farther
into her mass of hair. 'What is it called?'

'It's an allamanda,' Richard informed her, 'but anything else would have had the same meaning, tucked
behind your left ear. If you don't like the colour——'

'Oh no, it's beautiful!'

Richard smiled at her as they strolled back towards the
house, and for the first time since they arrived, she saw
him as belonging there among that exotic and colourful
background. Though it somehow served to make him
seem more distant from her suddenly. 'It looks a whole
lot more beautiful in its present setting,' he told her, and
one fingertip traced an imaginary pattern on her upper
arm as they walked. 'By the way, I haven't had much
chance to ask before—what did Adam have to say to you
after he got rid of me last night? Did he want to find out
if you'd try and talk me round to his way of thinking?'

'Apparently.' It wasn't a subject Willow wanted to discuss, but if Richard had realised after all that he had
been manoeuvred into leaving her alone with Adam, then
there was little else she could do but tell him what had
transpired. 'In fact he asked me to try and persuade you

to give up your music idea and join the company, but without success.'

'I could have told him that,' Richard declared confidently, and bent to kiss her mouth. 'I knew he wouldn't get to twist you around his little finger the way he does most women, you're too smart for him, and you don't see him the way most females do because you don't trust him.'

'I didn't say that!' Willow denied quickly, but Richard was shaking his head, and his smile suggested he knew better.

'I can tell,' he assured her confidently. 'But being Adam he just had to try—I know him!'

'Do you, Richard?'

Maybe it was something in the tone of her voice that made him look at her as he did and frown slightly. 'Why, sure I do,' he said. 'So why the heavy hint, darling?'

Willow shrugged. She just wished she found it as easy to shrug off Adam le Brun's failure to convince her as confidently as Richard did. Also she wished she hadn't let him see her doubt, because the last thing she wanted to do was discuss her talk with Adam last night. 'It wasn't exactly a hint,' she told him. 'I just think it's possible you don't know your brother as well as you think you do, that's all.'

'And what is *that* supposed to mean?'

Willow laughed shortly, seeing herself getting in deeper the more she said. 'I only wonder if you know to just what lengths he'll go to get you into the company, that's all. He's pretty determined.'

'And so am I!' Richard promised. Then he hugged her close for a moment and dropped a kiss on the top of her head. 'I'm not easily moved once I make up my mind about something; I'm that much of a le Brun, and Adam knows it. Also I'm certain Adam won't resort to anything too drastic once he realises I'm serious; you don't have to worry, sweet.'

'Maybe not.'

'Take my word!' But once again something in her voice must have betrayed her doubt and Richard looked down at her and shook his head. 'Willow, baby, I'd hate to think you don't like poor old Adam because of this; he's practically the only family I have, and I kind of like the old devil even if he is trying to hustle me into le Bruns by waving a big stick.'

'I don't dislike him.' Willow felt she could truthfully say that because whatever he might do or say, she felt she could never merely dislike Adam le Brun. He inspired much stronger reactions than that. 'It's just that he's such a—determined and ruthless man, the way I see him.'

'Sure he is, he's a le Brun!' Richard actually seemed to find her opinion of his brother amusing. For he was laughing as he bent to kiss her again. 'Just don't let him worry you,' he told her. 'He's not likely to try anything with you, especially as you've left him in no doubt at all that you won't try and talk me around.' He sounded so confident about it, Willow thought, that she simply hadn't the heart to tell him that he had already been proved wrong.

CHAPTER THREE

WILLOW had seen very little of the working part of the estate, mostly because Richard was not inclined to show it to her, although it was impossible not to notice the seemingly endless acres of pineapples that made up the biggest part of the property. And once, when they had been on their way into Honolulu, he had pointed out a huge building in the distance which he said was the le Brun canning factory, but it was obvious that he had no interest at all in the source of his family's wealth.

One day, Willow promised herself, she would get him
to show her more of what went on, because she did have
a genuine interest. But for the moment she contented herself with taking a walk as far as where the gardens of the
house ended and the commercial section began—acres of
red earth bristling with rows of spiky pineapples waiting
for harvesting.

It was probably with the idea of impressing Adam and
his grandmother that Richard had decided to put in a
couple of hours' practice with his guitar. He had told
Willow that he intended to spend two hours of every day
sitting in his room and practising, and it seemed not to
have occurred to him that by doing so he was leaving
Willow at rather a loose end.

She couldn't drive, or she might have borrowed a car
and gone into Honolulu, instead she had sat for nearly
half an hour in the shade of the porch formed by the
overhanging balcony, ostensibly reading a magazine.
But inactivity didn't come naturally to her, and she had
soon tired of doing nothing, and decided to take a
walk.

Having spent quite a lot of time enjoying the lush
beauty of the gardens she found herself at a narrow line of
palm trees that divided them from the pineapple fields.
Eventually, she told herself, she would venture farther,
and walk through the fields, but for the moment she stood
with her back to one of the palm trees, leaning against its
rough and slightly bowed trunk, grateful for its shade and
the cooling wind that came up from the not too distant
sea.

The thick fronds rustled like straw above her head and
through the thick feathery cover just one solitary beam of
sunlight managed to penetrate, winking on and off with
every play of the wind. It touched her cheeks with a warm
golden finger and made her smile, so that she lifted her
face and closed her eyes against its dazzle, leaning back
against the trunk of the palm with her arms pulled backward
around it, content for the moment to be where she was.

'Ah, a priestess of the sun!'

Willow flicked her eyes open and blinked for a moment in the bright beam of sunlight across her face. There could be no mistaking the voice, and she coped for a moment with an almost choking beat in her heart as she looked across at him. 'You startled me!'

It wasn't exactly a complaint, but Adam's mouth twitched slightly as he stood looking at her. 'Didn't you hear the truck?' he asked, and Willow shook her head.

'I didn't hear anything,' she confessed, and hastily looked away when he smiled again. Adam was the last person she wanted to see, but she couldn't simply walk away from him, so she stayed where she was and hoped he would go.

'Daydreaming, huh?'

'I suppose so,' she admitted reluctantly. 'These kind of surroundings encourage your mind to wander.'

Adam glanced over one shoulder at the field of pine-apples behind him. 'A pineapple paradise?' he suggested, but Willow merely shrugged, and hoped he didn't intend staying very long.

One hand was in a pocket and the other held a cigarette, and his eyes were narrowed slightly both against the upward rise of smoke and against the glare of the sun. There was a pair of sunglasses, she noted, tucked into the top pocket of his shirt. Light fawn slacks fitted perfectly over lean hips and long, muscular legs and the contrast of dark features with a snowy-white shirt was stunningly effective. It was quite absurd, Willow thought dazedly, the kind of wild emotions he could arouse in her, and, as she always did, she found herself resenting it.

'Do you have a special reason for lurking about down here on your own?' Adam asked, as if he had every right to question her movements, and she resented that too. 'If you're making for the beach you have a hell of a long walk in front of you,' he went on. 'I'd offer to run you down there, but I guess you're waiting for Richard to pick you up.'

It was very obviously meant to elicit the reason for her being there on her own, and for a moment Willow played with the idea of leading him on. Then she realised how easy it would be for him to discover she had deliberately lied, so she was driven to telling him the true situation, however reluctantly. 'Richard is going to be busy for the next hour or so,' she told him, and one dark brow flicked upward sharply.

'Busy?'

It was inevitable that she would be called upon to explain, and she flushed as she again averted her eyes, for she could almost guarantee that Adam would find something to mock in the idea of his brother practising so diligently. 'He's in his room, practising,' she told him, and the look she gave him dared him to find anything amusing about it.

'Ah, I see!'

A slow meaningful smile angered her every bit as much as she expected it would, and she shook her head. 'I doubt if you do!' she retorted. 'The fact is that it's necessary for him to practise, and he's made up his mind to do two hours every day.'

'For how long?'

'For as long as it takes!'

She bristled with resentment on Richard's behalf, and as she clasped her hands behind her tightly, encompassing the trunk of the palm, she was quite unaware for the moment of the effect it had of pulling the thin stuff of her dress taut over her breasts and hips. It was only when Adam's look made it clear he had noticed that she coloured furiously and hastily changed her position, standing upright and folding her hands together, low down in front of her.

'I just can't figure Richard,' Adam said, and smiled at her sudden hasty move as if it amused him. 'I'd have given him credit for more sense than to sit strumming his guitar when there's a beautiful girl to be had for the asking.'

'Not simply for the asking, Mr le Brun, make no mistake about that!'

Her eyes flashed green fire at him, and she saw the way his mouth pursed slightly, and the sudden heavy-lidded look about his eyes. Adam le Brun was a sensual man who made no secret of his desires, even when they involved his brother's girl, and her own emotions betrayed her again and again where he was concerned. Even after more than two weeks of living under the same roof, she was no more immune to his mature and somewhat earthy appeal than she had been at the beginning.

'He's a fool,' he declared in a deep quiet voice that teased her senses, and a look in his eyes challenged her to deny it.

But Willow was willing enough to take up cudgels on Richard's behalf, even if only for the sheer pleasure of defying him, and she glared at him angrily. 'Richard is *not* a fool,' she declared hotly. 'He's simply trying to show you and Madame le Brun that he's serious about his music. Give him credit for *something*; you're ready enough to condemn him for wanting to do something other than go into your company, you might at least be fair enough to acknowledge that he's working at it!'

Adam followed her example and moved into the shade, coming closer to where she stood and leaning against the tree beside hers, with one foot crossed over the other. She quite expected him to be angry, but instead he regarded her still with that faintly mocking smile. 'So he's doing it to impress us, is he?' he said. 'In the hope of making us see things his way, no doubt.'

Although she suspected that was just what Richard had in mind, Willow wasn't about to let Adam know it, and she shook her head. 'You just won't take him seriously, will you?' she demanded.

It was almost more than she could cope with, having to battle against the gamut of emotions that Adam aroused and at the same time try and defend Richard, and she hoped she could remain calm. She blamed him for trying to force Richard into a position he so obviously didn't want to be in, and worse, she resented his having tried to make her act for him. He was a dangerous and disturbingly attractive man, and she wished she was better able to cope with the effect he had on her.

'Why do you have to be so—so high and mighty about what Richard wants to do?' she cried in sudden despair. 'Why don't you just let him do what *he* wants to do? It can't make that much difference to your profits, surely!'

Ignoring the remark about profits, Adam eyed her for a moment narrowly. 'Is that what you think I am?' he asked quietly. 'High and mighty—is that what you think I am, Willow?'

'It's what you *are*!' Willow insisted, then wondered if she had at last gone too far.

But he still watched her steadily across the very short distance that separated them, then laughed shortly and shook his head. 'I can see why he brought you here,' he said with what struck her as dangerous calm. 'He needs your firebrand type of partisanship if he's going to defy me over coming into the company.'

'Nothing of the sort!' Willow denied recklessly. 'He's a grown man and he's chosen for himself; there's nothing you can do to stop him!'

She got the strangest feeling in the pit of her stomach suddenly when she noticed the way he was smiling. 'Isn't there?' he asked softly.

Willow was horribly uncertain what to do next, for she had a feeling that Adam le Brun knew exactly what he was doing, yet she was unwilling to relinquish the fight on Richard's behalf. 'I—I have to agree, with hindsight, that Richard probably did want me to come home with him because he needed moral support, but I don't blame him for that. Having met you I can see that he needs someone on his side!'

'Oh, you can?'

The quiet voice challenged her to go on, but Willow knew in her heart that she had already gone far beyond the normal bounds of behaviour towards one's host. There was little she could do about it now, but Adam le Brun was not the normal run of host either, and since he was unlikely to let her get away with anything, she might just as well go the whole way, having gone so far.

'You can't deny that you'd have bullied him into joining your wretched company by now, if I hadn't been here!' she declared, and Adam's eyes narrowed.

'I have no doubt of it,' he allowed quietly. Drawing hard on his cigarette, he stood looking at the glowing end of it for a moment before flinging it to the ground and grinding it under his heel. And there was something so incredibly ruthless about the gesture that Willow shivered, eyeing him warily when he moved closer suddenly. 'And you're encouraging him to go on with this guitar playing nonsense just for the sheer hell of putting one over on me,' he said softly. 'That about sums it up, doesn't it, Willow?'

Willow jumped quickly to her own defence, regardless of how close to the truth he came. 'I simply defend his right to do as *he* pleases instead of kowtowing to you, that's all!'

Having him so close reminded her of the occasion when he had tried to enlist her aid in persuading Richard, and something told her that he was of the same mind now. Knowing how possible it was, she felt her heart begin a rapid, thudding beat and her legs were shaking as if they could not support her for much longer. 'I wish you'd see reason,' Adam said, and the sound of his voice touched every nerve in her body.

'Reason being your way,' she guessed, and caught her breath when he closed the gap between them, the warmth of his bare arm brushing hers.

There was no way she could get away from him, she realised with a flutter of panic, for where could she go that he couldn't follow? And the pulsing warmth of his body so near recalled other sensations, like the strength of his hands and the fierce hardness of his mouth, so that she shivered as she stood, taut and expectant, waiting for him to touch her. When he did reach out with one hand and touch the small throbbing pulse at the base of her throat, his fingers were so light and gentle that at first she felt it as no more than a flutter of sensation on her skin.

'Why must you fight me so determinedly?' he asked softly, and Willow jerked up her head swiftly to deny it; met the shadowy grey eyes head on, and quickly looked away again.

'I—I don't fight you,' she whispered, and started visibly when he laughed.

'Oh, baby, God help me if you ever do!' His fingers stroked along the side of her jaw and he must have been well aware of the sensation he was causing. 'Why, you prepare for battle every time I come into the same room, and I can't help wondering why. Why must you fight me, Willow?'

'Adam, stop it!'

Jerking her head out of reach, she tried to disguise the fact that her self-control was rapidly slipping, though she had little hope with that narrow and infinitely disturbing gaze fixed on her. 'Stop it?' he echoed, and she bit anxiously on her lip.

'You're going out of your way to—to embarrass me, and if you're hoping it will make me more amenable where Richard is concerned, you're going quite the wrong way about it!' Her green eyes gleamed with a look of defiance, but they were defensive too, and she was in no mood for caution. 'Make things too uncomfortable for me here and I'll move out and into a hotel—then see how long Richard stays, after I've gone!'

'Blackmail?' The hand that swung her round to face him was far from gentle, and she shivered at the deep glow of anger in his eyes, held fast by her arm still. 'You dare to try and blackmail me, you——'

'Nobody?' Willow suggested rashly, and started at his harsh burst of laughter.

'Oh no, not that,' he denied softly, and curved his fingers more tightly into her arm, ignoring her complaint that he was hurting her. 'You couldn't be a nobody, Willow; you're more important than I'd figured if you really can influence Richard to leave home, and I have a nasty suspicion you could. But don't make threats like that, not when our family is concerned, there are too few of us.'

'I didn't——'

'Oh but you did,' Adam insisted quietly, 'and I promise you, Willow, that I make a very bad enemy.' He was so close that his breath warmed her mouth and the passion of anger was running close with another kind of passion that disturbed her much more deeply. 'The fact that you're a very beautiful and desirable woman won't make a scrap of difference; if you make any attempt to break up the family I'll make you very sorry, I promise you that!'

Willow did not understand herself. She was being threatened by a man who meant every word he said, she had no doubt of it, and yet she wasn't alarmed as she should have been, but strangely excited. And it was the look she saw in Adam le Brun's eyes that made her so. They glowed darkly, like storm clouds, but beneath the gleam of anger burned a raw and savage desire that kindled the most wild and primitive emotions in her.

Slowly she shook her head back and forth, trying desperately to keep her mind on less dangerous matters. 'I—I don't want to be involved in your quarrels,' she whispered. 'I didn't know what I was getting into when I told Richard I'd come with him; I wish I hadn't come.'

Adam's eyes bored into her, seeming to see right into her soul, and she shivered at the deep, husky softness of his voice. 'You don't mean that,' he told her. 'Do you, Willow?'

She didn't deny it because she couldn't, and she hadn't

come into the situation entirely unwarned. Richard had told her how autocratic his family was. She had expected Adam le Brun to be hard and relentless, and accustomed to to having things his way, but not for a moment had she anticipated that he would also be more attractive to her than any man she had ever met, and that he would, on occasion, make her forget Richard's very existence.

'Do you love him?'

The question startled her, and for a moment she simply stared at him, then she nodded swiftly and urgently. 'I'm engaged to him,' she said huskily. 'Of course I love him.'

'Engaged!' He looked down pointedly at her naked left hand. 'But not yet roped and branded,' he observed softly, and stroked a long finger down her cheek while his gaze moved upward to her copper-red hair. 'Your folks were way off target when they named you Willow, weren't they? I never saw anybody less cool and gently drooping than you.' He raked his fingers through the rich, bright strands for a moment, then gripped hard, with his palms resting on her cheeks. He drew her towards him and his words warmed her lips as he spoke. 'Look at me, Willow,' he whispered against her mouth, and in the moment she obeyed him he kissed her.

His mouth had a sensual warmth that stirred her blood, and it took hers with the same fierce confidence that she remembered from the last time he had kissed her. His hands slid down from her face to her shoulders and from there to the small of her back, bringing her deliriously close to the virile hardness of him, and she thrilled to the kind of excitement she had never known with Richard.

Richard sprang unbidden into her mind as she clung to Adam's pitiless mouth, and immediately her conscience banished the wild abandonment of the kiss. She tried to turn her head, but Adam's hand clasped the back of her head and held her firm, his long fingers gripping her hair and making escape impossible. Only when he allowed her to breathe again did she make another attempt to break away from him, but he looked down at her with the passion still burning in those no longer cool grey eyes.

He held her head between his hands as he looked down into her face, and Willow knew that he would take her mouth again if she didn't make a break right away. Struggling against his hands, she squirmed free, but her heart was hammering hard in her breast, and the act of pulling up her dress from her shoulder was entirely automatic. She was breathing hard and no one would have believed she was an unwilling partner, seeing her standing there in front of him, and shivering with a passion almost as fervent as his own, yet appalled to realise it.

Clinging determinedly to the thought of Richard, she turned swiftly and would have walked away without saying another word, but Adam's hand clamped firmly on her arm and stayed her, though she kept her back half to him, and didn't look around. 'Where are you going?' he asked in a voice that was harsh with emotion, and Willow shook her head.

'Back to the house.'

It was little more than a whisper, and his fingers dug deeper into the flesh of her arm for a moment. 'To Richard?' She shook her head quickly, and he turned her to face him again, though she came reluctantly. 'Shall I say I'm sorry, Willow?'

She didn't want him to be sorry, Willow realised dazedly, and shook her head again. 'Not unless you are,' she told him huskily, and Adam let his hand slide from her arm.

'I'm damned if I know whether I am or not,' he declared in a voice that was only slightly less confident than usual. As she still stood there, uncertain whether she should go or not, he ran a hand through his hair and slowly shook his head. 'I guess you'd best go and make sure Richard's still at his practice,' he told her, and Willow wished she didn't suspect him of feeling as guilty as she did herself. Men like Adam le Brun shouldn't have consciences, it spoiled the image.

One thing that made Willow's stay at La Bonne Terre less traumatic than it might have been was Madame le Brun's acceptance of her. So far the old lady had proved more amiable than she had dared hope, and she had even declared her intention of organising Willow and Richard's wedding, not for a moment considering that a le Brun marriage should take place anywhere but in their own domain. She had, it was true, qualified her interest by adding—'if it takes place'—but Willow suspected that had probably been done with the idea of quashing any impression that she might be softening.

For the past week, ever since that meeting with him in the palm grove, Willow had managed to avoid being alone with Adam, and she hoped she could go on avoiding him as much as possible. He not only disturbed her emotionally, but his present apparent uninterest in Richard's plans aroused her suspicion. She tried to tell herself that she disliked him, but in her heart she knew what she felt for Adam le Brun wasn't anything as mild as mere dislike. Virile and sensual and much more mature than she was, he made her feel that she could no longer trust her own feelings for Richard, and that troubled her.

Occasionally she sat with Richard while he practised, although the guitar as a solo instrument had never appealed to her, and he was less skilled than she expected, taking into account his plans to be a professional. But now that his mind was set on showing his family how serious he was about it he seemed little interested in anything else, and was less inclined to please her than to show his determination to become a musician.

Just at the moment, however, she had his undivided attention for once, and the conversation inevitably centred on his grandmother. 'I don't know how you've done it,' Richard told her, 'but she actually likes you.'

Willow laughed, seeing the observation as rather a backhanded compliment. 'I'm not sure that's very flattering,' she told him. 'But I think I know what you mean.'

'Sure you do.' He pulled a face, and Willow marvelled

at his almost childlike awe of his grandmother; sometimes
it even irritated her.

'You shouldn't let her see that you're so—overawed by
her, Richard. That's what makes her annoyed with you.'

'Plus the fact that I'm an international mongrel instead
of French,' Richard reminded her.

'Oh, nonsense!'

'Nonsense, hell!' Richard retorted. 'She never lets me
forget that my mom was a mixture of Irish, Italian and
English; I don't have any French blood from her at all,
and Grand'mère will keep reminding me of it till the day
she dies!' He kicked at the rug at his feet and his lower lip
was pursed disconsolately. 'I guess my yellow streak does
make her mad, but I can't help it. Old habits die hard,
and I've been scared of her ever since I can remember.'

'Oh, you do exaggerate!' Willow teased, and laughed
at his expression. 'If Adam isn't scared of her, why should
you be?'

'I guess because I *do* have a yellow streak where she's
concerned!'

'I expect Adam was just as much in awe of her when
he was a little boy, wasn't he?'

In fact she found it hard to visualise Adam as ever
having been in awe of anyone, even as a child, and
Richard shrugged. He had one arm resting along the back
of the settee behind her and his hand played restlessly
with her hair. 'I wouldn't know,' he said. 'He was already
nearly twelve years old when I arrived, and if he was ever
in awe of her he'd grown out of it by the time I was old
enough to notice.'

'Is he that much older than you?' Willow asked, and
did some rapid mental arithmetic. Richard was about a
year older than she was, and that made the gap between
her and Adam even more than she'd realised.

'It seems a hell of a lot when you're a kid,' Richard
said. 'And I guess we were never really so much like
brothers that we were company for one another. Then
when Mom and Pop died and he took over as a kind of

guardian, it made him seem even older.'

'It was quite a job for a young man,' Willow suggested. 'He couldn't have been more than twenty-seven or eight, and if you were sixteen——'

'You should get together with Grand'mère,' Richard interrupted. 'Join the Adam le Brun fan club!'

Willow flushed, there was nothing she could do about it, and Richard was looking at her curiously. 'Now you're being silly!' she told him.

'Am I?' He sighed deeply and, she suspected, insincerely. 'Anyway, she'd never see me in the same light she does Adam. For one thing I can't even speak good French, whereas he speaks it like a native after four years at a French university. I can't even get the accent in the right place.'

She found it hard not to smile at his determined self-pity. 'I can't say, because I've never heard you speak French, and I'm not expert enough to tell anyway. But I can't believe it has any bearing on the way your grandmother feels about you. She only gets a bit impatient with you because you let her see you're scared of her, that's all.'

His mouth drooping, Richard pressed on with his saga of woe. 'Worst of it is I begin to get the feeling that Adam shares her view of me, lately.'

'Oh, but he doesn't!' Willow declared impulsively, and realised only when she saw Richard's face just how confident she had sounded.

'No?'

'He's very, very fond of you, Richard, and very concerned about your future.'

'You sound as if you know that for sure,' Richard observed. 'It sounds very authoritative.'

He was watching her with the same kind of intensity that she associated more often with Adam, and Willow studied her hands rather than look at him. 'Hardly authoritative,' she denied, 'but I happen to believe it's true.'

'I'm just wondering how you can know how he feels.'

Foreseeing a few awkward moments because of her impulsiveness, Willow shrugged uneasily. 'I know because he told me.'

'Oh yeah?' Richard spoke quietly, and he turned suddenly and took both her hands. His voice reminded her a little of Adam's too and added to her uneasiness, 'And just why would Adam confide in you, sweetheart? What have you been at while I've been putting in my practice?'

'Don't be silly, how could I have been—at anything?' Willow declared hastily, and he laughed, a rather short laugh with an edge of harshness to it.

'It isn't so much you as that stiff-necked brother of mine that I suspect,' he told her. 'You can't blame me, after what you just said, for suspecting you've been having secret confabs with him, now can you?'

Willow hesitated. She could tell Richard that she had talked with Adam, but there could be pitfalls and if she let slip even a hint of what had actually happened out there in the palm grove Richard might be angry enough to make a break from his family, even if only temporarily. And she had been serious when she told Adam that that wasn't what she wanted to happen.

'There's no question of secret confabs,' she told him, treading very carefully. 'It was just that we got talking, that's all, and, not unnaturally, you were mentioned.'

'And the question of me joining the company came up again, huh?'

'Inevitably,' she said, and Richard was nodding as if something had suddenly become clear to him.

'Damn it, he's been putting pressure on you again! I should have known he wouldn't give up after only one try, that's not his way!'

Willow was anxious to impress on him that she had not been persuaded to Adam's way of thinking, and she shook her head. 'He didn't exactly put pressure on me,' she denied, 'and it wouldn't have done him any good if he had. I'm not easily pressured, Richard, and nothing Adam says will make me change my mind about not interfering; it's your decision and in the end you have to make up your own mind. I told him that the first time and I told him so again.'

But Richard seemed to have something else on his mind, and he regarded her narrowly, in a way that was discomfitingly reminiscent of Adam. 'If he didn't pressure you to do what he wants,' he said quietly, 'what *did* he do, Willow?' His hold on her hands tightened suddenly and she made a murmur of protest. 'Well, sweetheart?'

Willow tried to draw back her hands, and she looked at him reproachfully. 'I don't like being questioned as if you suspect me of conspiring behind your back,' she told him. 'I'm not a criminal, Richard.'

'Hell, of course you're not!' It was typical of Richard that he was immediately contrite, afraid of losing her sympathy, and he leaned forward and kissed her cheek. 'Baby, I'm sorry if I sounded suspicious, but I know Adam better than you do. I know what a two-timer he can be when he's out to get his own way, and I've spoiled his plans for having me join the company, so he's mad. But I swear that if he does anything to upset you I'll get out right now!'

'Oh no, please, Richard!' Willow felt a flutter of panic, for Adam would never believe she wasn't responsible if it really happened. 'Please don't say or do anything on my account that you'll regret. I'm sure Adam will see things your way sooner or later.'

Obviously unconvinced, Richard pursed his lips doubtfully. 'I can't see it,' he said, 'he's not an easy guy to convince, and he's real set on me joining the company. Unless——' He snapped his fingers suddenly, and the gleam in his eyes made her distinctly uneasy. 'Willow, baby, if you were to put in the word——'

'No, Richard!'

The very idea filled her with panic, but Richard ignored her objection and went on with his speculating.

'It might just work! He can't resist a beautiful woman, and you could, you just could pull it off, sweetheart.'

'Richard, no, I couldn't!'

Briefly he frowned his impatience. 'In heaven's name, why not?' he demanded. 'It'd do him good to have somebody play him at his own game.'

'I *won't*, Richard!'

'I don't get you,' Richard complained. 'Why won't you give it a try at least?'

Willow was shaking her head, bitter suddenly because no one seemed to take her feelings into consideration. 'Because I'm not some—object to be used by the pair of you to gain your own ends. First you did it, then Adam, and now you again.'

'Me?' His look of innocence did not for a moment convince her, and it was obvious from the way he avoided meeting her eyes that he knew exactly what she referred to. 'When did I ever ask you to help before now?'

'Do you think I haven't realised by now,' she asked with a hint of impatience, 'why you were so insistent that I come home with you? I'm not a fool, Richard, although I have to admit it took time to dawn on me.'

'I wanted to bring you home to meet the family,' Richard insisted, but Willow laughed shortly.

'You wanted me to act as buffer when you told Adam and your grandmother that you wouldn't be joining the company. Don't deny it, Richard.'

He said nothing for a moment, but sat with his right hand resting on the side of her neck and his fingers tangling restlessly in her hair. Then he met her eyes briefly with a look that was both appealing and defiant. 'O.K., I admit it,' he said. 'I'm sorry I didn't level with you, but I was scared you'd back off again if you knew, and I'd already had a hell of a time getting you to come as it was.'

'I would have thought twice,' she admitted reluctantly, and he nodded.

'There, you see! I guess I did hustle you a little, but

having you here to hold my hand when I broke the news wasn't the only reason I asked you, darling, you must believe that. I really wanted you to meet Adam and Grand'mère, and to see the old house; that's God's truth.'

She couldn't do other than believe him, and Richard could look very appealing when he wore that particular expression, so that Willow smiled almost without realising she did it. 'All right, I'll believe you,' she told him. 'But I wish you'd been more honest in the beginning.'

He leaned across once more and kissed her mouth, a light, lingering caress that stirred uneasy memories of another and very different kiss. 'I love you,' he whispered. 'I'd be lost without you.' With his forehead against hers he looked down at her for a moment, then brushed his pursed lower lip against her brow. 'You're sure you won't pressure Adam just a little on my behalf?'

'Definitely not!' She drew back and looked at him directly with her head on one side, wondering if he knew exactly what he was asking of her. 'Richard, what exactly are you asking me to do?'

He shrugged, obviously not quite with her. 'Put the squeeze on old Adam for me, what else?'

'The same way Adam wants me to—put the squeeze on you?'

'Yes, I guess so. Why not?'

Willow took a very deep breath. 'Adam wants *me* to persuade you because I'm engaged to you,' she told him, speaking slowly and choosing her words. 'Working on the assumption that I have ways of persuasion open to me that he doesn't have.' She raised her eyes and their green shadowy depths were filled with unmistakable meaning. 'Are those the kind of methods you want me to use on him, Richard?'

Realisation dawned at last, and Richard scowled. 'Hell, no!' he declared. 'You just have to—to talk to the guy, that's all!'

Willow smiled dryly and shook her head, wondering how he could be so ill-informed about his own brother.

'Adam,' she said with certainty, 'isn't the kind of man one just talks to.'

It was a couple of days later that Willow set out alone for a walk after having had a minor set-to with Richard. She was a little tired of him spending two hours and more every day in his room practising while she tried to find something to do with herself, and she had told him so when he suggested she sit with him.

In her own environment she wouldn't have minded nearly so much, because in familiar surroundings she would simply have found herself something to do and not bothered, but the le Brun household had its own routine and she was left to her own devices, making her feel still very much a stranger. Not that she suspected it was done with a purpose, because she was free to do as she liked and go where she liked, she only lacked company.

Without really planning anything, she set off on foot through the pineapple fields and in the general direction of a wooded crater that loomed over the slopes of the estate. The fruit flourished right to the very beginning of the wooded area, but it was quite a climb, and in her normal frame of mind she wouldn't even have considered it. As it was she saw the prospect of a long walk as an outlet for her annoyance, and the green wooded sides of the crater promised a different kind of outlook from any she had seen so far on Hawaii.

There were rough tracks running between the sections of pineapples, used by the trucks and the gangs of field workers, and by following one of them she came inevitably to the cool-looking woods higher up. She was wearing a sleeveless dress with a fairly low neck, but even so she was hot and sticky by the time she reached her goal, and breathing hard.

For the most part the trees were ones she didn't recognise, but they crowded close all the way up the steep slope to the very lip of the crater, and she welcomed the blessed cool of their shade with relief. A rough path of sorts ran upward and, having recovered her breath, she set out to follow it, drawn by some irresistible need to find out what lay at the end of it. Something she was never destined to discover, because she had gone only a short distance when her attention was caught by the sound of running water.

It was a matter of seconds only before the impulsiveness that had brought her on this trek in the first place turned her in the direction of the sound. It was a rock pool, Willow discovered after she had made her way through the brush and thick-growing trees, half hidden by the lushness of the vegetation and formed by a basin of hollowed-out rock, fed by a small cascade that probably came from the crater itself.

It looked deep and cool and inviting and quite irresistible, and Willow stood for a moment at its edge looking down at her own vague reflection shimmering among the green of the surrounding trees. There was a curious sense of stillness about it that was very relaxing, and after a moment she smiled down at her own reflection.

'Why not?' she whispered, and took a swift look around.

There was nothing and no one to be seen, and it was unlikely anyone would come, for it was far from the normal tourist places and the field workers were not likely to leave their work just yet. The tinkle and splash of crystal clear water and the enticing coolness of the pool itself eventually overcame whatever doubts she might have had, and with only a second's hesitation she began to strip off the few clothes she was wearing.

But even in these circumstances, a certain sense of propriety made her slip behind a beautiful red-flowered ohia tree while she took off her clothes, and she stood for a moment in her nakedness, contemplating the folly of what she was doing. Then, filled with a sudden sense of freedom, she stepped from behind the ohia and stood at the edge of the pool.

It was cooler even than Willow anticipated, but

beautifully relaxing once she got used to it, and after a couple of minutes she was swimming with leisurely over-arm strokes across the width of the pool. She felt a curious sense of excitement as the silky soft water rippled over her body; much more indolent and uninhibited, a woman who revelled in her own nakedness and the sheer primitive appeal of her surroundings.

With leisurely ease she made her way over to where the water came splashing down the rocks above, and after a moment she found a foothold that raised her waist-high from the pool and immediately under the cascade. Lifting her arms, she let the coolness of the water run down them and over her body, her red hair darkened and thinned by it as she closed her eyes and tipped back her head.

There were no other sounds but the soft splash of the water and the chittering of a bird somewhere in the bushes, yet when she glanced upward through the shim-mering fall of water over her face she caught a glimpse of a figure standing high up on the rocks above her, a tall, masculine figure, towering impressively over her own lowly position, until it disappeared almost before she had registered its presence.

Instinctively she stepped back into the deeper water again, shaking the clinging drops from her hair and lashes as she tried to see more clearly, treading water while she sought to still the sudden heavy pounding of her heart. Her whole body pulsed with a curious mingling of shock and excitement, and she couldn't imagine why she thought of Adam le Brun. It must simply have been a figment of her imagination; a mirage created by the effect of the shifting light on the water that ran down over her face. There was no earthly reason why Adam would have been there, and there was certainly no sign of anyone now, only the same bird chittering his complaint in the brush.

Nevertheless her heart was still beating faster than normal as she swam back across the pool to where she had left her clothes, and she had almost managed to convince herself it had been a mirage, when something heavy landed in the water beside her. It sent up a shower of spray that momentarily blinded her, then sank swiftly to the bottom, followed by Willow's dazed eyes.

Already at the edge of the pool, she clung to the rough rim of rock while she looked around her wildly, panic speeding up her heartbeat again, for there was no sign of a landslide, yet the missile that had so closely missed her had been unmistakably a piece of rock. There seemed a different atmosphere about her little paradise suddenly, and she was afraid without knowing why. Then something caught her eye, as it had done once before, and she looked upward to the overhanging rock cliff again.

Her vision was clearer now and she had no difficulty in making out the tall figure of a woman in a white dress; sultrily dark with blue-black hair drawn back from an oval face, and exotic almond-shaped eyes. It was the eyes that held Willow's bemused gaze, for they glowed with such undisguised malice it made her shiver, and as she watched, the woman bent to pick something up off the ground.

When she straightened up Willow caught her breath, for the woman held a massive chunk of rock in both hands. She stood for a moment looking down at her with those malignant dark eyes, then she raised her hands above her head. If Willow could have cried out, she would have, but she found it hard to believe that what she saw was actually happening, and she stared as if hypnotised at the tall, slender figure with the chunk of rock in her hands.

'No, Marsha!'

Willow blinked herself back to realisation when Adam le Brun appeared as if from nowhere and grasped the woman's wrists, and she watched the tussle up there on the rock with the feeling of watching figures on a stage. She found it hard to grasp that the minor drama taking place up there closely concerned her.

Shivering now with shock, Willow clung to the pool edge, and it was instinct pure and simple when she screamed as the rock came bouncing and clattering down the slope and fell with a great splash into the water immediately below the waterfall. There followed a breathless kind of silence that was quite uncanny, and then Adam's voice, sharp and anxious.

'Willow?'

When the spray cleared he could see her again, and she did not turn her face but kept her back to him, not even raising a hand to acknowledge his unspoken question. He could see she was unhurt, and she was only waiting now for the two of them to leave. A sudden scrabble of movement and the sound of receding voices, sharp and quick with anger, told her that she was alone again, and she bent and laid her forehead on her wet arms for a moment.

She was shaking like a leaf and her teeth were chattering all the time she brushed the water from her body with her hands and put on her clothes again, and she did not see how she was going to face Adam again. Richard must never know about it, she had already decided that, and if she could she would take care never to see Marsha Sia-Hung again, for she had no doubt that her assailant had been Adam's determined woman-friend.

She made her way back along the path, but hesitated to emerge from the sheltering trees because she had the discomfiting feeling that Adam would be there. Far along on the dusty track between the rows of pineapples she saw a car being driven so recklessly fast that it racketed from side to side and raised a cloud of dust that virtually hid it from sight most of the time, and she guessed Marsha Sai-Hung had lost the battle if not the war.

As she half expected, there was a le Brun truck parked right up under the trees with Adam at the wheel and obviously waiting for her. When she didn't come to him, he came to her, and his hand on her arm was so light and gentle that she felt very small and vulnerable suddenly, for it seemed like a reminder of what he had seen from up there above the pool.

'I'll run you home,' he said quietly, but Willow instinctively shook her head.

'There's no need,' she denied. 'I can walk.'

'Maybe,' Adam conceded coolly, 'but in the circumstances I think you'd be better off riding. Let's go, eh?'

Because Willow felt as she did, she turned on him swiftly, seeking to bring up the matter she knew must be as much on his mind as hers, rather than hide behind an uneasy silence. 'You think I did wrong to bathe in that pool?'

His coolness somehow made her more agitated, for he seemed so completely untouched by the episode she half resented it. 'Not at all,' he told her. 'I'm only sorry Marsha showed up, I wasn't expecting her.'

'How did she know?'

Her voice sounded small and hesitant, and Adam's fingers pressed slightly into her arm. 'I noticed you coming and thought I'd better warn you about possible pitfalls on the crater,' he said. 'I followed you, and Marsha must have followed me; I guess we both got a surprise.'

Willow had allowed herself to be led across to the truck despite her expressed opinion, and by now she was feeling a little less shaky, although she still didn't meet his eyes. 'That was Marsha Sai-Hung?' she asked, and Adam looked down at her and raised a brow.

'I suppose Richard told you about her,' he guessed, and she nodded. He saw her into the truck and slid into the seat beside her, then turned in his seat, studying her for a moment with an expression Willow found hard to interpret. Then he cupped her chin in his hand and lifted her face to him, his strong fingers gently insistent when she tried to resist. 'What exactly did he tell you about her, Willow?'

Willow didn't reply at once. She would rather have been making her own way back instead of sitting in the truck, half stifled by the heat in the cab and too aware of a warm, masculine scent that set her pulse racing. 'He told me that she's made up her mind to marry you,' she said, recklessly uncaring who she upset.

'Oh, he did!'

Willow gave him a long look from the corner of her eyes. 'From the way she went on just now, I'd say he's right,' she told him, and it was a second or two before she realised he was laughing.

The warmth of his body brushed her soft curves as he leaned forward slightly and brushed strands of dark, wet hair from her face and she shivered without realising it. 'Richard should give more time to looking out for you instead of taking wild guesses at my future,' he said quietly. 'I guess he left you to your own devices again, eh?'

'He's practising.'

'Not at being a fiancé,' Adam remarked, and it was automatic for her to go to Richard's defence when she noticed the small half-smile on his face.

'He has to practise if he's to get anywhere, it's obvious.'

'Ah-hah!'

The ball of his thumb moved lightly back and forth across her lips, and to Willow his nearness was the temptation it always was. It made it harder to forget he had seen her standing naked in the rock pool, but the initial shock had now become a feeling of inevitability. Adam le Brun made her feel that he knew her better than any man ever had before, and she felt he accepted her nakedness as a natural fact in the circumstances; he wouldn't dream of trying to apologise or make excuses, because it would make her more selfconscious.

'I've said it before, he's a fool,' he told her softly, and his thumb over her lips made it impossible for her to protest. 'He should stick with you and make sure you don't come to grief in a strange place.' When he looked at her his eyes were heavy-lidded and sensual and they moved slowly over her face until they fixed immovably on her mouth. 'If you were mine I'd make sure you didn't go swimming alone, I'd go with you.'

Flushed and trembling, Willow shook her head, trying

to banish the picture she had of that long, lean body cleaving through the crystal clear water of the pool beside her. Hastily she jerked her head aside but kept her eyes downcast. 'But I'm not yours,' she reminded him. 'If I'm anybody's, I'm Richard's.'

Adam fixed his eyes on the quivering softness of her mouth again, then he leaned forward, bringing his body into even closer contact and touching his lips to her mouth. 'Then I guess I'd better drive you back while we both still remember it,' he murmured in that devastatingly soft voice, and kissed her hard before turning away to start the engine.

CHAPTER FOUR

IT seemed to Willow that nothing was ever going to be quite the same again between her and Adam, and she did her best to avoid him, although it wasn't easy. At mealtimes he was always there, for one thing, and each time she noticed those dark-fringed grey eyes looking in her direction she was reminded of her rashness in bathing naked in the rock pool. In some curious way she felt she would have been less troubled about it if Marsha Sai-Hung hadn't seen her too, for the woman's reaction suggested the kind of nature that would not easily forget.

She felt sure Richard would never learn about it from Adam, any more than from her, but she was less certain what Marsha Sai-Hung would do if the opportunity arose for her to make mischief. It was for that reason that Willow found herself with rather mixed feelings about going with him to what Richard described as a *luau*. Everyone would be there, he assured her, and everyone, she assumed, would include Adam and Marsha Sai-Hung.

'It's a real Hawaiian do, darling,' he told her, his eyes beaming with enthusiasm. 'I know you're not much of a partygoer from choice, but you'll enjoy this, it's different from anything you've ever been to before.'

'It sounds it,' Willow agreed cautiously, and Richard leaned closer, encouraged by her faint smile.

'This won't be one of those clambakes put on for the tourists,' he promised. 'The Kimurazes are one hundred per cent *kamaaina* and so will everybody else be but you. You'll be the only *malihini* there, simply because you're my *wahine*.'

Willow knew exactly what was expected of her, and she was ready to play along if it amused him. He wasn't in the habit of sprinkling his conversation with Hawaiian expressions, and she half smiled as she looked at him enquiringly. 'All right,' she said, 'so tell me what all that means.'

'Sure!' From the way he was smiling it was obvious she had said the right thing. '*Kamaaina*, that's me and Adam and anybody else who was born here, right? It means islander.'

'And Madame le Brun?'

'Well,' Richard allowed with a grin, 'I guess you could count Grand'mère as *kamaaina* after eighty years. You, on the other hand, count as a *malihini*—an incomer or stranger.'

'And *wahine*?'

He leaned and kissed her, his eyes bright and teasing. 'Woman,' he said. 'You're my woman.'

'I see.' They sat together on one of the garden seats and Richard was holding her hands, half turned to face her on the seat. 'And after we're married do I become a *kamaaina*, or shall I still be a—whatever else you said?'

Watching him, Willow realised that he had suddenly become withdrawn slightly, as if mentioning their marriage made him uneasy, and she could not imagine why it should. 'I guess you'll still count as *malihini*,' he said eventually, and that hint of distance was still there so that she regarded him with her head to one side, although she said nothing about it at the moment.

'Well, I suppose that's fair enough,' she conceded. 'But tell me more about this party. Where is it to be?'

He brightened immediately, his smile as warm as ever. 'The Kimuraz place, out near Mua beach.'

'I suppose I shan't know anybody, shall I?'

'You'll know Adam,' Richard told her, confirming her initial doubts. 'And it will be your chance to meet Miss Fu Manchu.'

Willow's heart gave a sudden and violent lurch, even though she had expected it. 'You mean Marsha Sai-Hung?'

'Who else?' Probably she had spoken more sharply than she realised when she mentioned Marsha Sai-Hung, for Richard was eyeing her curiously. He knew nothing of her dramatic introduction to Adam's woman-friend, of course, but every feature of that smoothly malicious face was indelibly imprinted on Willow's mind and she shuddered. 'You don't have to look like that, sweetheart,' Richard told her with a laugh. 'Even Marsha observes the social niceties at a do like that; just don't glance in Adam's direction, give her a clear field, and she'll purr like a cat.'

'I have every intention of keeping clear of her, don't worry,' Willow assured him.

But she shuddered inwardly when she recalled the sheer hate in those almond eyes as they looked down at her, and the great clumps of rock that came hurtling down into the pool, much too close for comfort. Even fully dressed she couldn't hope to remain unrecognised, and she felt far from as certain as Richard seemed that Marsha Sai-Hung would keep a rein on that venomous temper of hers once she recognised her.

'I don't know that I'm all that keen on going,' Willow demurred, but Richard wasn't going to have his plans spoiled without very good reason, and she could hardly give him the true one in the circumstances.

'Oh, come on, sweetheart,' he coaxed, giving her cheek a swift peck. 'You aren't that shy, and besides, I want to show you off. I've told them I'm bringing you and they're looking forward to meeting you, so you're sure of a welcome. This isn't one of those deadly things where you stand around with a glass in your hand hoping to find someone to talk to, this is a real Hawaiian *luau*. You'll love it.'

'If you say so.' She was weakening, and he knew it; Richard was never in any doubt about his powers of persuasion.

'Forget all about Marsha,' he told her firmly, and squeezed her hands tightly. 'I'll be there to hold your hand, and I promise that if we see Marsha lurking behind a jacaranda I'll defend you with my life. O.K.?'

But what would he do if he knew that her safety, if not her life, had already been threatened by the woman's jealousy? Willow wondered. She hesitated for a moment, then realised that she couldn't go on making excuses without arousing his suspicion, so she gave a little laugh and shrugged.

'O.K.,' she agreed. 'How do I dress for this do? Not in a grass skirt, I hope!'

'It's a great idea,' said Richard, satisfied with the outcome, 'but your prettiest dress will do. It's informal, but I want you to knock their eyes out, baby, so make it something special.'

Smiling faintly, Willow nodded. 'I'll do what I can,' she promised.

'That's my girl!' He leaned across and kissed her mouth with more enthusiasm than finesse. 'I knew you wouldn't let me down!'

Nor would she let him down, Willow thought, as she eyed herself in the bedroom mirror on the evening of the party. Following his instruction she had put on her prettiest dress, and the result was better than she expected. It was deep jade green in colour and had pleated half-sleeves and a low neckline, and it was flattering in more ways than one.

Its soft lines flattered her figure, and its colour did wonders for her creamy skin and copper-red hair. It guaranteed she would be noticed, even among a crowd of brightly dressed Hawaiians, and it crossed her mind briefly, as she turned away, to wonder what Adam would think of it; a dangerous thought that she hastily dismissed as she closed the bedroom door behind her.

Downstairs in the *salon* she had to pass a much more critical test than Richard was likely to put her through, and Madame le Brun's sharp, dark eyes noted the flush in her cheeks as she paraded rather selfconsciously before her. Approval came eventually with a brief nod, and she was called across to sit next to the old lady, encouraged by a smile that was a curious mixture of mischief and warmth; a smile that Willow was growing accustomed to.

'You know how to dress,' the old lady told her with her customary frankness. 'That colour is perfect for you and you're clever enough to know it.'

Willow smiled. She was, in fact, becoming quite fond of the autocratic old lady who sat in her high-backed chair as if it was a royal throne, and already she stood in less awe of her than Richard did, who had known her all his life. When she glanced briefly at her wrist-watch, Madame le Brun noticed that too, and nodded.

'Don't fret, child,' she advised her. 'He won't keep you waiting, unless he's a bigger fool than I take him for.'

Willow ignored her sharpness and smiled once more. 'I'm not fretting, Madame le Brun; Richard's pretty punctual as a rule.'

'Always ready to defend him,' the old lady said, and there was a shrewd glint in her eyes for a moment. 'But I guess you can count on him keeping close to you tonight at the Kimurazes, because there'll be plenty of roving eyes there, and if he doesn't watch it some other *kanaka*'ll come along and take you away from him!'

'Oh, that won't happen,' Willow assured her. 'He's promised to hold my hand all evening.'

The sharp old eyes narrowed for a second and regarded her steadily. 'You sound as if you might be scared of something or somebody,' said Madame le Brun, 'and I can't imagine why a girl like you should be scared. Why do you want your hand held? What are you nervous of, girl?'

Keeping her eyes downcast because that shrewd, sharp gaze was still on her, Willow shrugged lightly. 'Nothing, *madame*. I'm not scared, it's just that I shan't know anybody—except Adam, of course.'

At that Madame le Brun's eyes narrowed a little more. 'Has Richard been telling you about Marsha Sai-Hung?' she asked, and Willow looked up swiftly and involuntarily. 'Ah, I see he has! Well, you have no reason to be scared of her, child, unless you try getting too friendly with Adam, and I can't say I've noticed you pay him any particular attention. Still, if you've heard about Marsha, you'll know how things stand.'

Richard had suggested that his grandmother was dead set against any idea of a match between Adam and Marsha Sai-Hung, heiress or not, and hearing her seemingly accepting their affair as a fact aroused violent and unexpected resentment. It was pure instinct that made Willow react as she did, and she took no account of the impression she might make.

'I know how Mrs Sai-Hung would like things to stand,' she said. 'I'm not at all sure that Adam thinks along the same lines!'

For a moment the old lady's eyes gleamed between their sparse lashes, but her sudden low chuckle was completely unexpected, and Willow flushed when she suspected its cause. 'Oh, I see,' Madame le Brun said. 'So you think Adam is being hustled and you don't like the idea, is that it?'

'I didn't say that, *madame*!'

'It's obviously what you think,' Madame le Brun retorted. 'But what interests me is how you can sound so sure what Adam thinks.'

'I—I don't.'

'Do you have good reason to believe he has other ideas?' the old lady demanded, ignoring her denial completely.

'None at all, *madame*. He neither confirmed nor denied it.'

Willow was flustered or she would have realised how much she was giving away, and she bit anxiously on her lower lip as she sat flushed and uneasy under the old lady's shrewdly sharp gaze.

'So he's talked about it,' Madame le Brun said softly. 'You surprise me, girl, I hadn't imagined you and Adam as being on confidential terms. But I guess you're a whole lot deeper than you seem at first glance; redhaired women are always deep.'

Willow said nothing, but she heaved an inward sigh of relief when Richard at last put in his appearance. He looked sleek and incredibly handsome in a white suit and a blue and white patterned shirt, and he pursed his lips when he caught sight of Willow. His silent whistle was endorsed by the gleam in his blue eyes as he took in every detail from head to toe.

'Will I do?' she asked, slightly breathless, and Richard took both her hands and drew her towards him.

'Baby, you really *will* knock their eyes out!' he breathed, and kissed her soundly as if he was oblivious of his grandmother's speculative gaze. When he raised his head he looked directly at the old lady and there was a bolder air about him this evening; a certain gleam in his eyes that belied his professed fear of her. 'If we go now we'll beat old Adam to it,' he said, but Madame le Brun was shaking her head at him.

'He's already left,' she told him, 'just before Willow came down.' There was a look in her eyes that made Willow curiously uneasy, for she switched her gaze from Richard to her as she spoke, as if she thought the information of more interest to her. 'I expect he went to pick up Marsha.'

Something in her manner must have struck Richard too, for he gave Willow a brief, curious glance before looking at his grandmother again, and there was a slight frown between his brows. 'That figures,' he said. 'I guess we'd better get going too or I'll have to drive too fast for Willow's liking.' He gave the old lady a light kiss on her cheek and a faintly impudent smile. 'Don't wait up, Grand'mère!'

He was silent while they walked out to the car, though he smiled as he saw Willow into the passenger seat, and he brushed his lips lightly across her forehead before he closed the door. When he slid in beside her, Willow looked at him curiously, for she felt sure he had something on his mind, and she had a feeling it concerned her.

'Is it far?' she ventured, and Richard shook his head.

'Down nearer town.' He was quiet again, then he half turned his head and looked at her. 'What were you and Grand'mère talking about when I came in?' he asked.

Wary, without quite knowing why she had need to be, Willow shrugged. 'Nothing much. She asked if I knew about Marsha Sai-Hung, then guessed you'd told me about her.'

Richard pulled a face. He guided the car along the wide, busy highway with his usual panache, but his mind was on something else, and Willow wondered why he was so interested in what she had been discussing with his grandmother. 'She didn't ask when we were getting married?' he asked suddenly, and she was surprised enough to stare at him for a second or two.

'No,' she said eventually. 'Although it wouldn't really be surprising if she did, would it, Richard? She does take an interest, you know, and she seemed much more ready to accept me than you led me to expect.'

'She's taken to you,' Richard observed, and something in his tone suggested that his grandmother had not come up to expectations by taking a liking to her.

'Isn't that to the good?'

It was only a very short silence, but to Willow it seemed meaningful and she felt a slightly faster beat in her heart as they turned off the highway suddenly and drove along a smaller, tree-lined road. Then he turned his head and beamed her one of his bright, confident smiles. 'Sure it is,' he agreed. 'I'd looked for opposition all the way, and instead she takes you to her heart, as if she'd chosen you herself.'

'Which is a relief to both of us,' Willow suggested quietly, and once more felt a faint twinge of uneasiness when he didn't answer.

Big, opulent-looking houses stood well back behind their own lush little paradises and every variety of shrub and tree that grew at La Bonne Terre grew here, surrounding the houses of the rich in this luxurious suburb of Honolulu. A car preceded them in through a wide gateway and along a shrub-bordered driveway, and another followed them, so that it seemed the guests were arriving thick and fast.

Fairy-lights were strung from all the trees, and the sound of singing voices and Hawaiian guitars reached them the moment Richard cut out the engine, as well as a babble of talk that even the open air failed to dim. As he helped her from the car Willow felt her pulse beating hard and fast, and when he looked down at her and smiled she responded with a smile equally warm, for she was infected by her surroundings already. It was her first Hawaiian party, and she wasn't going to let Marsha Sai-Hung or anyone else spoil it for her.

Richard seemed to have recovered his usual brightness too as they made their way round to the back of the house where the feast was to be held, and he explained something of what was going on. It appalled Willow at first to learn that two deep pits had been dug in the immaculate lawn, and these were the *imus*, or underground ovens where the food had been cooking for most of the day.

Two whole pigs, scrubbed, seasoned and wrapped in wire netting, were buried in the pits along with red-hot stones, sweet potatoes, plantains and various little parcels of meat and fish; it would, he assured her, be like nothing she'd ever had before. But although Willow announced

that it all sounded rather primitive and not very appetis-
ing, the general atmosphere of the party was irresistible,
and she found herself infected with the same excitement
and sense of anticipation as everyone else.

Sitting at the long, low tables provided for the feast wasn't
nearly as awkward as Willow had expected it to be, even
though she was squashed against her neighbour on either
side with barely enough room to use her arms. She was
seated about half way along one table with Richard on
one side of her and a tall, handsome young Polynesian on
the other, and several times during the meal she was
reminded of Madame le Brun's remark, when the man's
dark, admiring eyes made it plain that if Richard neglected her he was more than willing to take his place.

The traditional way to eat *kalua* pig, so Richard had
informed her, was with the fingers, and Willow found
herself becoming quite adept at it as the meal progressed.
All she had to do was to pull the tender meat into small
pieces and pop them into her mouth along with some *poi*,
which at first she had eyed with distaste. It was a sticky
brown paste into whose origins she didn't enquire too
closely, but which didn't taste as bad as she expected, and
also had the advantage of helping to stick the pieces of
meat to her fingers. It was messy but fun, and she enjoyed
every mouthful once she got the hang of it.

The number and variety of side dishes was staggering,
and these were for the most part unfamiliar, but Willow
didn't let that put her off. Mixtures of salmon and tomato,
chicken and coconut, and a dark and rather unappetising-
looking mollusc referred to as *ophi*, all accompanied the
succulent pork, and somehow all tasted good together.

Willow had carefully and deliberately avoided looking
for Adam, but it was inevitable that sooner or later she
would spot him, and the feast was well under way when
she noticed him sitting at the same table but some distance
along on the other side. Just as inevitably he had Marsha
Sai-Hung beside him, sleek as a cat in a yellow silk dress

that fitted high at the neck and skimmed the curves of her voluptuous figure lovingly close in all the places that mattered. Her intriguing eyes were on her food at that moment, but would undoubtedly note any move of Adam's to acknowledge her.

In the act of popping in another mouthful of pork and *poi*, Willow happened to catch Adam's eye and the gleam of laughter she saw there brought a quick warm flush to her cheeks, for she was all too familiar with that faint hint of mockery. It was pure instinct that made her wrinkle her nose at him, while at the same time she licked the sticky *poi* from her lips with the tip of her tongue in such a way that it appeared she was poking it out at him.

His sudden burst of laughter was spontaneous and uninhibited, and he was shaking his head at her when Marsha Sai-Hung looked up. Her lips tightened into a thin line that had all the sharpness of a trap, and her beautiful dark eyes narrowed to mere slits. If only Adam hadn't seen her. Willow thought ruefully, or else she had had the sense not to provoke his laughter with that vaguely childish display, Marsha Sai-Hung might have overlooked her, despite that other occasion. As it was she could feel the other woman's fury searing across the distance between them, and she instinctively leaned a little towards Richard.

He turned at once and smiled down at her. 'O.K., darling?' His enquiry was casual, and Willow nodded, licking *poi* from her fingers. 'Know what?' Richard went on, very obviously pleased with himself. 'I've been promised I can sit in for a couple of numbers with the band later on; Sammy Kimuraz fixed it for me. I guess that'll give old Adam something to think about, eh?'

'That was lucky for you.' It was a break for him and he was quite naturally pleased about it, but to Willow it meant that yet again she was to be left to her own devices, just as she was when he practised at home. 'Just for a couple of numbers?' she asked, and Richard grinned and winked an eye.

'With a bit of luck I can do the rest of the evening,' he told her, and obviously hadn't given a thought to her situation. 'I never expected a break like this, sweetheart, not for a hell of a long time yet, but when Sammy invited us and said the bandleader was a buddy of his—well, it was too much to pass up.'

'But you didn't think to tell me about it until now.' She tried not to sound too complaining and spoil his pleasure, but didn't altogether succeed, and Richard looked vaguely uneasy.

'I figured you might not come if you knew,' he confessed, and Willow pulled a face.

'Very likely,' she agreed dryly. 'Oh well, I can always find myself another partner, I suppose. According to your grandmother I shouldn't have any difficulty.'

'Oh, Willow!'

He looked reproachful, and Richard was very good at looking reproachful. He could made her feel she was being hard and unfeeling, when she knew in her heart that she was nothing of the kind. But he wanted to play in the band and she hadn't the heart to stand in his way, however she felt. 'All right,' she said, trying not to sound and look too sorry for herself. 'I suppose you're going to finish your meal first, though, aren't you?'

'Sure I am!' He was so obviously pleased with himself again now that she had conceded. 'I don't reckon to lose out on any part of this,' he assured her. Which, Willow recognised ruefully, probably summed up Richard's attitude to life in general.

It was, in fact, almost another hour before he took his place, rather selfconsciously, among the players in the band, and by then the loaded tables tables had been reduced to a chaos of food scraps and mangled blossoms, and the guests were drifting towards an area of the garden laid out as a dance floor. He was using a borrowed guitar and seemed far more nervous than Willow would have expected him to be, but she gave him a kiss for luck, and hoped he wouldn't notice that she moved away after his first number.

There were plenty of people who would have been willing to keep her company, but she felt strangely alien among all the smiling faces, and instead she decided to seek out the cool, quieter places in the gardens, and enjoy her own company for a while. Soon lost in the now familiar fragrances, she walked along a winding, shrub-bordered path, not much caring where it led her, and the farther she walked the more distant the sound of the music became.

At the end of the path, where it branched off into another, stood a row of lofty jacarandas, looming like grey ghosts in the moonlight, and fluttering their fern-like leaves against the night sky. Without benefit of sunlight the bell-shaped blue flowers appeared darkly colourless, yet were still somehow quite beautiful.

Instead of taking the alternative path, she pressed on beyond the row of jacarandas, finding that the shrubs grew much more thickly there and that there was no path to follow. So that before very long the going became quite difficult and she began to realise that pushing her way through as she was wasn't doing much good to her dress.

Nevertheless there was a curious kind of tranquillity in that miniature jungle, and she only reluctantly turned to retrace her steps, catching her breath swiftly when she heard a sound in the bushes. It sounded like someone else making their way through the tangle of vegetation, and since she could only assume that someone had followed her, she felt a sudden flutter of fear. One hand to her throat, she stood for a moment with her eyes darting around the close growing shrubs in search of whoever it was.

'Willow—did I scare you?'

When Adam appeared as if out of nowhere she closed her eyes briefly in mingled relief and alarm, for the last time she had seen him Marsha Sai-Hung had been beside him, and she couldn't believe she was very far away now. 'I—I didn't expect to see anyone else.'

It annoyed her to realise how small and unsteady her voice sounded, and her heart gave another leap in her breast when he moved through the bushes towards her. It was hard to interpret his expression, for his eyes were hidden by the shadow of dark lashes, and the contours of his face appeared strangely enigmatic.

The cream suit he wore had the effect of making him appear even taller than usual, and even in the uncertainty of moonlight she noticed a small pulse at the open neck of his shirt beating hard and fast. Adam never failed to affect her in a way no one else ever did, and in this particular situation she was edgily wary. Still waiting for Marsha Sai-Hung to come after him, so that she started with a fluttering of hands and lashes, when he spoke again.

'Richard's a fool! I guess he's trying to prove something by getting up there and playing in the band, but leaving you alone is neither smart nor polite.'

'I don't mind!'

She came to Richard's defence automatically, as she almost always did, and she saw the brief twitch of Adam's mouth as if it amused him. 'Don't talk such nonsense, Willow—of course you mind!'

That deep and alarmingly affecting voice caressed her like a stroking hand, and she shivered. Then, because she needed something to distract her, something to take her mind off Adam and the sheer excitement of his proximity, she reached out and pulled a blossom from a melia tree growing right alongside her, holding it to her flushed cheek for a moment. Its incredible fragrance added another touch of magic and her heart was beating so hard and fast that she could hear it like a drumbeat in her head.

'He couldn't turn down a chance to play in public with a professional band,' she said, fighting hard to keep her mind on more practical matters, although it wasn't easy with that dark, enigmatic face before her. 'You—you can't blame him, Adam.'

'I blame him for leaving you on your own.' He moved

closer, and Willow caught her breath. She clasped the flower she was holding so tightly that the stem snapped suddenly and the head fell to the ground at her feet. Her distress was exaggerated, because she was so emotionally disturbed, and Adam bent at once and retrieved it, holding it in his hands for a moment before he reached over and tucked it into her hair, just above her left ear. Then he smiled faintly and looked deep into her eyes. 'It suits you,' he said softly.

He didn't remove his hand, but rested it lightly on her neck, and the warmth of his palm brought an even harder beat to her heart. 'Richard says a flower tucked behind the left ear means I'm spoken for,' she ventured, and noticed one dark brow arch swiftly.

'Then it's a pity he doesn't remember it,' he said.

Willow was trying desperately to control her racing pulse, but even the mention of Richard couldn't change the effect Adam had on her, and she despaired of her own weakness. 'It's a beautiful perfume,' she said, in a voice barely above a whisper.

'You're a beautiful girl.' He stroked his fingertips lightly on her neck, and Willow shivered, keeping her own eyes downcast so that she need not see the look in his—that deep, darkening look of desire that she had seen there before, a look that took no account of her relationship with Richard, but burned into her senses and brought a response she could do nothing to control. 'How could anyone be such a fool as to leave you to go and play in a band? Didn't he realise how you'd feel at being—discarded?' The deep soft voice went on, soothing but at the same time stirring those alarmingly wild emotions into being again. 'Is that why you came and hid yourself away in here, Willow? I saw you coming this way——'

'And followed me!'

Her voice trembled and sounded strangely husky as Adam lifted a thick tangled mass of copper-red hair and tugged it gently. 'I followed you,' he conceded softly, 'because I thought I knew how you must be feeling.'

'It was kind of you.' Willow looked up and her eyes were huge and dark in the moonlight, for she didn't believe kindness was his only motive, and Marsha Sai-Hung still lurked uneasily in the back of her mind. 'You—you weren't alone either,' she whispered, and once again she noticed that brief twist of amusement on his mouth.

'Marsha got cornered by our host about something they both feel strongly about,' Adam told her quietly. 'And I'm not on a leash, Willow, never think it!'

'I don't!'

So he had escaped Marsha Sai-Hung to come and find her, but for how long remained to be seen. He said nothing for a moment, but stood with his hand still resting on her neck and his strong fingers wound into her hair, pulling back her head slightly. Then he drew her towards him, his free arm binding her close and his hand just lightly resting on the curve of her breast. There was a thrusting hardness in the body that pressed against her own gentle curves, and the same gleaming look of desire burned into her as she tilted back her head and offered him her mouth.

He took it with the same almost savage fierceness as before, and her own desires stirred and responded with an abandon she had never known except with him. Everything else was banished from her mind but the hard, passionate body that aroused and released emotions that had no place in her normal quiet, ordered existence. She lifted her arms and pressed the softness of her body to the hard, demanding virility of his, and her lips were warm and eager and willingly given.

'Adam——'

It was several moments before she had breath enough, then she spoke in a small and very unsteady voice that she scarcely recognised as hers, and looked up into the deep, stormy greyness of his eyes. She was warm, yet she was shivering, and the only thought in her head was to bring that hard, stunning mouth down to hers again.

'Willow, for the love of God, give him up before you get hurt!'

The shock of the words stunned her for a second, so that she stared up at him with blank, unseeing eyes, then she shook her head slowly. She had expected endearments, whispered entreaties, after a kiss like that, almost anything but that harsh order concerning his brother, and she swallowed hard on the frantic beat of her heart as she eased herself away from him.

Both the words she needed and the breath to say them were hard to come by, but eventually she managed them, though her body still pulsed wildly with the heat of passion he had aroused in her. 'I—I was wrong to let this happen,' she whispered, 'but that doesn't mean I don't——'

'If you're going to say you're in love with Richard, don't!' The harshness of his voice belied the look in his eyes, and Willow was shaking like a leaf as she stood in front of him with her hands clasped tightly over one another. For a moment he simply stood looking at her, then with one hand he lightly touched her cheek, and no matter how she blamed him for his severity concerning Richard, Willow thrilled to the touch of him as she always did. 'I guess you're still young enough to be in love with love,' Adam told her softly, and the harshness was gone from his voice, leaving that deep, soft timbre that could always be her undoing. 'Admit it, Willow, why don't you?'

'I won't admit it because it isn't true!' Hysteria edged her voice, and she tried hard to control it. 'I've admitted it was wrong of me to—to behave as I did just now, but it doesn't make any difference to the way I feel about Richard!'

A passion of some kind still showed in Adam's eyes, and he looked at her with an intensity that she found almost frightening. 'And just how do you feel about Richard?' he asked quietly.

In a sudden onset of panic Willow realised that she was no longer sure exactly how she felt, but she wasn't going to let Adam know that. 'I'm going to marry him,' she insisted shakily. 'I'm engaged to him, that's the only reason I came all this way with him!'

'And the fact that he's not only good-looking but also a very good catch,' Adam suggested, and Willow's reaction was swift and instinctive.

Her hand connected with the tanned smoothness of his cheek with more fury than she realised, making him shake his head in surprise, then a sudden wild surge of emotion rose in her and spilled over as she took to her heels and ran. She went roughly in the direction of the house, but she had no real clue to where she was going as she flitted like a pale ghost between the trees, and Adam's voice followed her, thick with anger.

'Willow!'

But Willow neither paused nor slowed down until she reached the row of jacarandas, and only then because her legs felt too weak to carry her much farther. The tangle of voices was closer now, and the strumming harmony of the band, reminding her that Richard was unlikely to be available with a comforting arm. Her heart was pounding unmercifully hard, and a small, sharp pain in her side caught at each breath she drew in.

Somehow she must have taken a different turning, for she found herself not among the crowd on the lawn at the back of the house, but in the quiet of the front drive among the parked cars, where a fountain played peacefully into its stone basin. Even here shrubs and trees grew in the same profusion, and light streamed out from the house, but it was quiet and secluded, and that was what she needed at the moment.

While she tried to get her breath back, she stood by the fountain's stone basin breathing heavily, with the back of one hand pressed to her mouth and her eyes blinking anxiously as she took stock of her situation. Adam le Brun wasn't the kind of man to easily forgive such an assault, even though he had provoked it, and the fact that Willow considered he had deserved it would have no bearing on his reaction. The marks of her fingers would remain visible for some time, and even he would think twice about reappearing among the other people while they still showed.

Because it was so quiet at the front of the house the sudden slight sound of footsteps on the driveway behind her made Willow turn swiftly, thinking it might be Adam. The backs of her legs were pressed against the fountain's edge and she swayed slightly with the impetus of her turn, staring in stunned dismay when she found herself facing Marsha Sai-Hung.

The smoothly beautiful face was virtually expressionless, but Willow felt a sudden flick of panic when she met the dark eyes and recognised a certain gleam of triumph. The yellow silk dress caught the light and made her gleam like an Oriental goddess, and she moved towards her with the lithe grace of a cat, and a faint smile on her mouth.

'I guess you're Willow Grahame.'

The voice was smooth and soft, but the strong American accent came as a surprise somehow, and Willow nodded automatically. It was simply because she wasn't thinking too clearly that she spoke as she did. 'And I know you're Mrs Sai-Hung.'

The dark eyes glowed and her smile became wider, showing small, perfect teeth. 'I'll bet you do,' she drawled. 'I can imagine Richard has had plenty to say about me, and you'd better believe it, Miss Grahame!' Her gaze didn't shift, yet she gave the impression that she was checking to make sure they were still the only ones on that side of the house. 'What else did he tell you, apart from the fact that I know how to take care of myself?' she asked, and Willow understood at last what Richard meant by saying she purred. Her voice had just the velvet softness of a cat purring for Marsha Sai-Hung was enjoying herself, and it was that that made Willow so anxious.

'Only that you're—a friend of Adam's.'

'A friend?' The smile widened. 'More than a friend, Miss Grahame; which is why I don't take to the idea of smart little cookies like you making a play for him.'

Not normally afflicted with cowardice, Willow actually

toyed with the idea of ducking out and running as fast as she could in search of Richard. But both Richard and his grandmother had seemed certain that Marsha Sai-Hung wouldn't show her claws too openly on an occasion like this, and she feared she was over-reacting.

Flicking a moistening tongue over her dry lips, she shook her head. 'I haven't made any play for Adam, Mrs Sai-Hung,' she denied. 'I'm engaged to Richard.'

'So I hear!' The dark eyes mocked her. 'But I'll bet Richard doesn't know you go sneaking off to swim in the nude, does he, honey? I'll bet he doesn't know you paraded in the buff in front of Adam, like a downtown stripper, does he?'

Willow was appalled to realise she was colouring furiously, and she shook her head. 'I had no idea Adam was anywhere near!' she protested.

'I'll bet!'

'It's true! Do you think I'd have stripped off if I'd known there was anyone to see me, and especially Adam?'

'Especially Adam.' The words were repeated softly, and the beautiful almond eyes narrowed slightly as Marsha Sai-Hung advanced on her, bringing the strong scent of jasmine with her as well as the brittleness of hate. 'So you count Adam as somebody special, do you?'

'I—I just meant that——'

'I can guess what you meant,' Marsha Sai-Hung told her. 'Well, you like the water, Miss Grahame, so you enjoy yourself!'

The words had scarcely time to register before a long, slim hand slapped hard on Willow's shoulder and sent her spinning backwards; toppling her over the edge of the fountain and into the splashing chill of water. She cried out entirely by instinct when she landed on her back in about nine inches of water, and floundered desperately for a moment or two before she realised that there was absolutely no danger. Then she grasped the edge of the stone basin and hung on, crying in sheer desperation. She didn't even notice Marsha Sai-Hung go back to the party, but for a moment she hated Adam with as much venom as his lady-friend hated her.

CHAPTER FIVE

WILLOW found it hard to explain, without going into detail, exactly how she came to fall into the fountain, but she was insistent that she did *fall* in, and so far only Richard had openly expressed doubts. Kitty Kimuraz, their hostess, had been so charmingly concerned and helpful that it was hard to believe she was Marsha Sai-Hung's cousin. It was difficult to imagine how two women who looked so much alike could be so different in character. No questions had been asked, but while she was drying off and being given a change of clothes, Willow was several times made aware that Kitty Kimuraz regarded her curiously.

She had seen nothing of Adam since last night, but it was too much, she suspected, to expect he would let her get away with slapping him, and she felt that with one thing and another she had just about as much as she could cope with at the moment. She had attempted to pass off Richard's curiosity without telling him what had actually happened, but he was being particularly insistent.

'I just don't get it,' he said. 'You weren't sloshed, I'd swear to it, so how could you just—fall in? The damned thing's big enough to see, and there was plenty of light— it doesn't make sense.'

'Well, I *did* fall in, and that's all there is to it,' Willow told him with a touch of impatience. 'If you'd been there to dance with me I wouldn't have been wandering about on my own like an old-fashioned wallflower!'

'Ah, poor baby!' He leaned and kissed her lightly just below her ear, but Willow suspected that his apology was merely a form of lip-service. 'Don't take swipes at me, darling, you know I'm crazy about you.'

'Then why don't you spend more time with me?' Willow insisted. 'I don't expect to be inveigled into going to a party where I know virtually nobody, and then be left to my own devices while you go off and enjoy yourself. At least I can sit back and relax when you disappear all day at home to strum your wretched guitar.'

'Not *all* day, baby,' Richard protested, and from his expression her dissatisfaction with the way things were came as a surprise. 'Only long enough to impress Adam with the fact that I'm serious, even to the point of neglecting you.'

'You think it'll make any difference?'

Richard shrugged. 'I hope so.'

'So you mean to go on neglecting me?'

'Ah, darling!' He hugged her close for a moment, and to her dismay Willow found herself comparing his almost casual embrace with Adam's fiercely possessive one. But it was dangerous to make comparisons, she knew, and she immediately shrugged off the thought. 'I tell you what,' Richard said, breaking abruptly into her thoughts. 'To make up I'll give you dinner in town tonight, how about that?'

'It sounds fine,' Willow told him with a glance from under her lashes, 'just as long as you don't leave me to eat alone while you go and join the band.'

'Ah, baby!'

His eyes were reproachful, and because she hadn't intended to complain quite so determinedly about his practising, Willow shook her head. 'I'm sorry, Richard, I know you have to practise. Where are you thinking of taking me tonight?'

'Let me choose, huh?' She nodded, and Richard bent his head and kissed her, both arms wrapped around her as he looked down into her face. 'I guess I deserved to have you chew my ear for neglecting you,' he conceded with one of his engaging grins. 'Even old Adam has noticed it.'

'Did he say he had?' Willow wondered if he noticed her stiffen slightly when he mentioned Adam, and she tried to sound matter-of-fact. 'I can't imagine why Adam would be interested in how I feel.'

'Don't kid yourself,' Richard retorted. 'He knows that the way you feel affects me, and he's interested in anything or anybody that influences me!'

Willow recalled Adam's sudden and unexpected advice to her last night, to give up Richard before she got hurt, and that didn't exactly fit in with Richard's notion. 'He knows I don't try to influence you,' she objected. 'I told him that right from the beginning, when he tried to get me to talk you into joining the company. What you do is your own affair.'

'Maybe. But according to Adam I'm asking for trouble where you're concerned, going on as I am. I mean, leaving you alone while I practise. He says that if I got smart and joined the company you wouldn't be left to your own devices so much, and you wouldn't get fed up—you know how he goes on.'

'But as far as I can see it wouldn't make much difference if you did change your mind,' Willow observed, and he frowned at her curiously. 'From what I've noticed,' she went on, 'Adam is away for most of the day, most days of the week, and I can't imagine that you'd be given any more free time than he is.'

'That's a point,' Richard mused thoughtfully, and his eyes narrowed. 'Do you suppose the old devil is trying out a policy of divide and conquer? Maybe he figures that if he scares me with the prospect of you getting fed up enough to pack up and take off, I'll change my mind about joining the company. Next thing he'll be working on you, suggesting how neglected you are, and how much better off you'd be back home!'

Willow was studying the pattern on his shirt rather than look at him, for he came too close to the truth for comfort, and it occurred to her that Adam's policy might well be to divide and conquer. His apparent concern that she might get hurt was probably nothing more than an attempt to get her to leave, and had nothing to do with her feelings at all.

'I'm rather surprised he doesn't know by now that by threatening you he'll only make you dig your heels in harder,' she said. 'You wouldn't simply give up, even if I did go home, would you, Richard?'

Briefly he tightened his arms around her, then he laughed suddenly and buried his face in her hair. 'Oh, you wouldn't leave me, darling, I know better than that!' He kissed her with his usual brash confidence, but when he looked down at her she detected a faint glimmer of doubt in his eyes. 'Would you?' he insisted.

Willow traced the pattern of his shirt with a fingertip and chose her words very carefully. 'Not without very good reason,' she said.

'You promised to stay at least until fall,' Richard reminded her. 'You wouldn't run out on me before.'

'Not unless, as I say, I had very good reason,' Willow agreed. She could feel the intensity of his gaze as she kept her own eyes downcast still, approaching a subject she always felt curiously hesitant about discussing with him. 'I would like to be able to tell Madame le Brun a definite date for the wedding, Richard. She's always asking me when it's to be and I feel a bit silly having to tell her I don't know.'

'I don't see why,' Richard declared, and recognising a trace of irritation, Willow shook her head.

She wasn't altogether happy about Richard's attitude towards any mention of their marriage plans. He hadn't even bought her an engagement ring yet so that sometimes she wondered if it hadn't been a mistake to agree to the very tentative arrangement that was all that existed between them at the moment. 'It makes it very awkward for me,' she told him quietly, for heaven forbid that he should think she was pushing too hard.

Richard was frowning, and the arms around her were

almost brutally tight, as if tension made every muscle as taut as a spring. 'But what's the hurry?' he demanded, and Willow shook her head.

'None as far as I'm concerned,' she assured him, still in the same quiet and carefully controlled voice. 'As I told your grandmother, neither of us is in any hurry, but naturally she's interested, and I think she's getting a bit impatient.'

'Let her!' Richard declared shortly. 'It's our affair, not Grand'mère's!'

Then he hugged her closer suddenly, and rested his chin on the crown of her head, but Willow would have given much to be able to see his eyes at that moment. It was true, what she had told Madame le Brun, neither she nor Richard was in any special hurry to marry, but in fact she more and more believed that it was more true of Richard than of herself, and his present attitude seemed to confirm it.

'If only you weren't so old-fashioned, my darling,' he murmured, his lips brushing her cheek. 'There wouldn't be any need for wedding bells. You know I love you, and you say you love me, but the minute I ask——'

'We've been over all this a hundred times before,' Willow interrupted in as steady a voice as she could manage, 'and the answer is still no, Richard.'

It was true, they had argued about it from every possible angle, and so far neither of them was prepared to budge an inch in the other's direction, and somehow lately Willow had been more sure than ever that she never would change. 'I know you always say no,' Richard murmured coaxingly, 'but——'

'But nothing,' Willow insisted. 'It may seem old-fashioned to you, Richard, but that's the way it is. Now please don't ask me again.'

He sighed deeply and looked as vaguely sulky as he always did after losing the interminable argument that he always lost. But Willow knew that he would come around, and very soon—he always did, for he was nothing if not optimistic, and sure enough he looked up suddenly and caught her eye.

'O.K., have it your way,' he conceded, then bent and kissed her mouth, laughing as he looked down into her eyes. 'But don't think I've given up!'

'You might as well,' Willow told him, but nevertheless found herself tempted to smile.

'You've got a thing about wedding bells,' he teased, and kissed the tip of her nose. 'But let's have a little fun first; dine, dance and make merry, eh, sweetheart?'

'Why not?' Willow agreed, readily enough, but once more she recalled Adam's injunction that she should break off with Richard before she got hurt. It came as something of a surprise when she found herself seriously considering doing just that.

Willow had left the choice of restaurant entirely to Richard, and she had no complaint to make so far. It was situated right in town, but had a setting as lushly exotic as anywhere on the island, and it offered a mixed menu of Hawaiian and more ordinary dishes. The little tables were set among willow trees and alongside a fish pool, and massed shrubs gave an illusion of privacy even when the place was crowded.

Guided by Richard, Willow chose something he called *laulaus*, which turned out to be very similar to the little parcels of fish and meat she had eaten at the party the night before, and just as delicious. She followed them with a huge portion of coconut pie, and did as several of the other diners were doing, threw scraps into the pool for the fishes to eat.

She couldn't help noticing how free Richard was with the wine they had with their meal, but he was enjoying himself and there was no reason why he shouldn't drink more than he normally did, if that was what he felt like. Looking across at her, his blue eyes were bright and had an almost unnatural glow in the soft lighting, despite the fact that his expression was deadly serious.

'You look very beautiful,' he murmured, and got to his feet, leaning across the width of the table to kiss her hard on her mouth, regardless of the attention he attracted and the smiles he raised. 'I love you, my darling.'

Flushed and rather selfconscious, Willow shook her head. 'I don't mind you kissing me in the least,' she told him with a slightly unsteady smile, 'but not in front of a restaurant full of people, Richard.'

'Why not?' he demanded, and his voice was plenty loud enough to be heard by those sitting nearest. 'I don't care if people see me kiss you.'

'Put it down to my British reserve, if you like,' Willow told him, unconsciously keeping her own voice low. 'I prefer being kissed somewhere a bit more private.'

'Prissy!' He mocked her slight frown exaggeratedly. 'O.K.—so you don't like being kissed in a restaurant. Let's go outside and I'll kiss you where it's dark, if that suits your British reserve better! If you've finished your coffee, let's go, eh?'

His mood troubled her slightly, though Willow told herself that he was simply a bit over-exuberant after a good meal and rather too much wine. Nevertheless she got up from the table with deliberate slowness, so as not to suggest she was making a hasty retreat. Richard was pretty well known, but even though he called greetings to several people on their way out, he didn't stop to introduce her, and Willow was conscious of curious and speculative eyes following her as they left.

'You know a lot of people,' she ventured as they emerged into the cooler outside air, and Richard laughed.

'And they're every one of them trying to figure out who you are,' he said, apparently finding the situation to his liking. Then he laughed again as they crossed the car park, and clasped her arm more tightly. 'I feel like I'm walking a foot above ground, and I'm made of candyfloss,' he told her, and Willow eyed him doubtfully when he almost tripped, and gripped her with both hands for a moment while he recovered his balance.

'I'm not surprised,' she told him. 'You started off with two whiskies in the bar and then had the lion's share of the wine!'

'Now, now,' Richard admonished with mock severity. 'No sly little digs, darling—you did your bit too.' He turned her to face him and held her by both arms while he looked down into her face, and there was a sly little half-smile on his mouth. 'Is the parking lot private enough for you?' he teased. 'You look all shiny-eyed and beautiful, and I'm going to kiss you even if the whole goddam population of Honolulu is looking on!'

Willow laughed, for there was something irresistible about Richard in this faintly mocking and mischievous mood, and it was true that she had drunk quite a bit more than she normally did. The effect, however, was rather pleasant, and now that she was out in the fresh air everything and everybody seemed so much more bright and beautiful than before, so that she smiled and swung her copper-red hair about her face as she looked up at him.

'I *feel* all shiny-eyed,' she told him, then giggled and added, 'Adam wouldn't approve of this at all, would he?'

Willow couldn't imagine why she had seen fit to mention Adam at that moment, and Richard was looking down at her and frowning. 'Adam?' he said. 'What made you suddenly think about Adam, for Pete's sake?'

Wishing that she hadn't let her tongue run away with her, Willow shrugged uneasily. 'I don't know,' she confessed, and giggled. 'I suppose he just sort of popped into my head, that's all.'

'Well, sort of pop him out again,' Richard ordered solemnly. 'He'd go bananas if he knew I was driving home feeling the way I do right now, but he isn't going to know, so what the hell!'

In fact it wasn't until that moment that Willow had given much thought to driving home, and the prospect sobered her a little as she looked at him. 'Maybe you shouldn't drive,' she suggested. 'We could get a taxi——'

'Not on your life!' Richard declared indignantly. He stood beside his car with one hand holding the keys and the other arm around her shoulders, and his eyes shone darkly blue in the light from the overhead lamps. It struck Willow, as he stood there, that in this light he looked very much more like Adam than she had ever noticed him before, but she quickly banished the insistent thought of Adam yet again. 'Don't tell me you're scared of driving home with me,' Richard challenged, and laughed as if the very idea was ludicrous.

But Willow considered it very seriously for a moment, then she shook her head. She wasn't thinking clearly, but something at the back of her mind warned her that Richard was in no condition to drive them home, and she ought really to tell him so. But he was looking down at her and his blue eyes were shining, and in the end she simply hadn't the heart to refuse him.

'Just take it easy,' she warned. 'Please, Richard.'

'Don't I always?'

He swept her against him suddenly, with such force that the breath was knocked out of her, and his mouth came down on hers in a long, hard kiss that had little of love or gentleness about it, but stirred certain reactions in her, despite herself. 'Oh, sweetheart,' he murmured against her mouth, 'if only you'd let me——'

'No!'

'O.K., O.K.!' His laughter teased her and he kissed her again, even harder. 'O.K., you little puritan!'

Why, Willow thought dazedly, did his kiss do so much to remind her of how much more exciting Adam's kiss had been last night? Somehow she just couldn't seem to get Adam out of her mind, and it was almost as if thinking of him had summoned him up, for from the corner of her eyes she saw him come into the car park. It seemed inevitable that Marsha Sai-Hung should be clinging possessively to his arm, and Willow disengaged herself with indecorous haste when she saw them.

'What's wrong?' Richard demanded, then he too spotted his brother, and laughed softly. 'Well, what d'you know?' he drawled, and there was an unmistakably malicious gleam in his eyes as he watched them coming their way. 'Big brother and Madame Fu Manchu are on the town as well!' Looking around him at the rows of parked cars, he spotted Adam's and laughed shortly when he recognised it. 'Why in hell didn't I recognise his car when I parked?'

'Maybe they came after we did,' Willow suggested. She was feeling strangely small and vulnerable as she stood there with Richard and watched Adam escorting Marsha Sai-Hung, but for some curious reason she prickled with resentment too. 'Richard, why don't we go?'

'And let him think I'm running away?' Richard's smile mocked her, and his voice was unnaturally loud and bright so that it betrayed his over-indulgence all too obviously. 'Let's stick around and find out old Adam's opinion of us—it could be fun.'

Had it been possible, Willow would have got into the car and avoided becoming involved in the kind of confrontation that Richard had in mind, but she had little choice. Richard's arm was firmly around her shoulders and the car was still locked; there was no way out for her, and she already felt herself shrinking from the anticipated mockery in Marsha Sai-Hung's eyes.

Unlike Richard, Adam was in formal dress, and the white dinner jacket seemed to give added severity to the lines of his face as he drew close enough to recognise his brother's condition. At first he merely nodded to them, and Richard looked vaguely disappointed, but the moment he had seen his companion safely into her seat he turned back to them. It looked, Willow thought a little dazedly, as if he wanted to make sure that Marsha Sai-Hung took no part in whatever was to come.

Then he turned his eyes on Willow, and their expression showed that he knew she had been imbibing too, so that to her annoyance she found herself meekly lowering her eyes before his disapproval. It was several seconds before he gave his attention to Richard, and she noticed how disturbing that quiet, deep voice of his was, even in these circumstances.

'I hope you're not thinking of driving home, Richard,' he said, and Richard frowned, as if a direct attack wasn't quite what he expected.

'Sure I am,' he insisted. 'Why not?'

'If you need to ask,' Adam told him, 'you definitely shouldn't drive.'

'Are *you* stone cold sober?' Richard demanded, and it was clear that whatever amusement he had hoped to derive from the situation had been overcome by resentment, and he looked flushed and angry.

'Near enough,' Adam told him, and again turned his gaze on Willow's flushed face before going on. 'And if you don't care about your own thick hide, at least think about Willow.'

It startled her to hear him use her to strengthen his argument, and Willow had to admit that she saw his point of view, but the inevitable effect he had on her senses aroused unexpected resentment in this instance, so that she came automatically to Richard's defence. 'I'll be perfectly safe, Adam——'

'You take care of your girl and I'll take care of mine,' Richard interrupted shortly. Then he grinned and bowed low in the direction of Adam's passenger, a mocking gesture that cost him a bang on the head when he collided with the roof of a neighbouring car. 'Whoops!' he laughed. 'Hang on there, Rich!'

'For God's sake take a cab home,' Adam urged him. 'Or let me drive you. You're not fit to drive, Richard!'

'So you already said,' Richard reminded him, 'but I've got five bucks says I can make it without even taking a wrong turning! You'll trust me to drive you home, won't you, darling?' He smiled down at her confidently, but when Willow opened her mouth to declare herself less sure than she had been, he promptly kissed her before she could utter a word. 'Willow isn't scared, she knows I'm not drunk!'

'You're drunk enough to be dangerous,' Adam insisted shortly. 'And if Willow wasn't in much the same state, she'd realise I was right.'

'I am *not* drunk!' Willow declared indignantly. 'You have no right——'

'Are you thinking of slapping my face?' Adam asked, very softly and with unexpected malice, so that she caught her breath. 'For heaven's sake,' he went on with a sudden burst of impatience, 'do something to discourage him, Willow!'

It was hard not to do as he said, and try, for that wonderful voice always had an effect on her, but she felt curiously helpless at the moment. 'I couldn't even if I tried,' she told him, and just for a moment while she held his eyes, her legs trembled alarmingly. 'We'll be O.K., Adam; we're neither of us as drunk as you think.'

For a long moment Adam looked across at her steadily and she found herself wishing that he would insist on her riding with him, though she refused to admit that it was because she so disliked the idea of him taking Marsha Sai-Hung home. Then she noticed that he was slowly shaking his head at her. 'You little idiot,' he said at last, softly but with a hint of steel in that velvet voice. Without another word he turned and got into his car, and Marsha Sai-Hung's faint smile was the very last straw—Willow hastily turned her back.

'And don't try tailing me to keep an eye on us!' Richard yelled in tipsy bravado. It was obvious that he saw his brother's withdrawal as a tactical victory, and Willow had to agree, although she recognised that without her connivance there was little Adam could have done. 'We're taking the inland route so you'll be long in your little bed when we come home!' was Richard's final shot.

Adam said nothing, but his face had a dark threatening look that sent shivers of sensation up and down Willow's

spine. Last night she had slapped him, hard, and tonight
Richard had forced him to back down, and Adam le Brun
wasn't the kind of man to take that kind of treatment
without doing something about it. Just briefly he turned
his gaze on her again, and his eyes glittered and gleamed
in the harsh yellow light, then he drove off with Richard
waving him a mocking farewell.

Richard was laughing when he turned back to her, well
pleased with himself, while Willow felt anything but
happy about the way things had turned out. 'Shall we
go?' Richard bowed her with exaggerated courtesy into
his car, and she glanced at his smiling and good-looking
face with a fluster of apprehension as he closed the car
door on her. The encounter with Adam had sobered her
considerably, for he had brought it home to her just how
unfit to drive Richard was. However, she had burned her
bridges, and there was nothing she could do about it now.

It was a beautiful night, and driving along the narrow
inland road back to La Bonne Terre Willow began to
relax a little, and to enjoy the sensation of driving through
completely strange moonlit countryside, despite some
heart-stopping moments as the car climbed the rough hill
road and the bends became more tortuous, the land
dropping away sharply on one side. The advantage of going that way was that there was virtually no traffic, but
it was unlit, and more than once she gripped the car door
when Richard took a particularly nasty bend at speed.

He was still feeling elated over his victory, and he
turned his head every so often to smile at her, laughing
when she discouraged an attempt to drive and put an
arm around her at the same time. The moon was full,
and every bit as big and romantic-looking as the Hawaiian
moon was supposed to be, and it shed its radiance over
everything, making the hilly landscape look softer and
more beautiful.

'It's—it's so lovely,' Willow said, and didn't understand
why she sounded so wistful. Sometimes the island confused
her utterly, consisting as it did of ultra-modern American

and ancient Hawaiian, but it intrigued her too. 'In the moonlight it's quite beautiful.'

'So are you,' Richard replied promptly. 'But you sound kind of mopey, sweetheart. You're not sorry you let me drive you home, are you?'

Giving him a sideways glance from the corner of her eyes, Willow's raised brow expressed her feelings. 'Not yet,' she told him.

'Aw, come on,' Richard objected, and turned his head to look at her. 'If you're going to be nasty to me I shall hurl us both to destruction over that cliff.'

'You'll do it whether you mean to or not if you don't keep your eyes on the road,' she told him. 'I wish you wouldn't keep turning your head, Richard.'

He showed his excellent teeth in a wide smile. 'I can't help it, you look like you're not quite real in this light.'

'I shall look even less real spread all over the landscape,' Willow told him, and pulled a face. 'For heaven's sake, Richard, slow down a bit!'

'Chicken!' His smile mocked her, but Willow was again hanging on to the car door, her anxious glances on that ominous drop to their right.

'Please, Richard, there's another car in front, and there isn't room to pass on this road!'

'Ah, leave it to me!' He made no attempt to slow down, but peered through the darkness at the vehicle ahead, and barely picked up by their headlights as yet. 'Now who else is on this li'l ole dirt road at this time o' night?' he mused, then gave a sudden wild yell of triumph that startled her so much she gasped aloud. 'It's Adam!' The gap between the two cars was closing rapidly and Willow too recognised the one in front as Adam's. She could even recognise the silhouette of his head outlined by their headlights, and her heart started a hard, urgent hammering in her breast. 'He's dropped Marsha off and he's taken the hill road to see if he can sneak up on us,' Richard guessed, and his sudden chuckle stirred cold little chills in Willow's stomach. 'O.K.! If that's what he wants, we'll give him a run for his money!'

'No, Richard!'

She didn't realise quite how anxious she sounded, but something in her turned icy cold at the thought of giving chase and trying to overtake that familiar car with Adam at the wheel on this narrow, dangerous road. Her mind flitted back over the memory of strong brown hands, and she imagined them wrestling desperately with the steering-wheel as he fought to keep his car on the road and avoid either colliding with his brother or tipping over that stark, steep cliff.

'Oh no, Richard, please don't!'

Richard, however, was in no mood to be frustrated, to be deprived of one more victory over Adam, and he put his foot down hard. 'Move over, big brother,' he shouted. 'Here we come!'

The car in front seemed to loom at them with heart-stopping speed, almost on their front bumper, and Willow put a hand to her mouth. 'No, don't, Richard!'

Some instinct had warned Adam, for he turned his head for a second, a swift jerky movement that showed just how startled he was, then he signalled urgently for them to slow down. 'Not on your life!' Richard yelled at the top of his voice. He gave a bloodcurdling war whoop and the big car hurtled past his brother's, almost brushing it in passing. 'Geronimo!'

They were careering into another bend almost immediately, with the brakes hard on and the tyres squealing, and Richard's hands were suddenly taut on the spinning wheel, as if he fought for control.

To Willow it was a jumble of sounds heard all at once, and then, suddenly, she felt herself snatched from her seat and hurled into the air, with her own voice shrilling in her ears as if it belonged to someone else. There was a sensation of cool, rushing air, then a thud, and she lost consciousness.

It was over an hour later before Willow began to take

conscious notice of anything again, and then it was a
glimpse of white overall coat and a smiling face that encouraged her to open her eyes wider. 'Oh, good, you're
back with us,' the white coat said with obvious satisfaction, and Willow did her best to respond to the smile of
the woman who wore it.

She held a card in one hand and the other hand was in
the pocket of her coat. 'You're Miss Grahame, right?' she
asked, consulting the card, and Willow inclined her head
slowly.

'Willow Grahame.'

'That's a cute name, and kind of pretty,' the woman
told her in a soft, Oriental-sounding voice. 'I thought the
Chinese were the ones who used those kind of names.' She
pulled a face, and Willow noticed vaguely that she had
slightly almond-shaped eyes and a smooth oval face.
'Would you believe I'm called Little Flower in Chinese?'

'It—it's pretty.'

Willow was doing her best to respond, but she felt a
cold sensation in her stomach that grew more insistent as
she lay there, and the voice was suddenly more brisk and
clinical when it returned to the business in hand. 'Well,
now that you're feeling a little more lively, shall we see
what has to be done?'

Willow barely heard what she said, for she was desperately trying to recall exactly what had happened, and as
her memory slowly surfaced, she turned her head anxiously in the direction of the door. 'Adam,' she said faintly.
'I must know——'

'You just quit worrying about anybody else at the
moment,' the brisk but kindly voice told her. 'Concentrate
on *your* troubles.'

'But I *am* worried,' Willow insisted, and would have sat
up except that the moment she tried her head began to
spin round and round, and it felt as if there were hundreds
of tiny hammers beating painfully at her temple.

'Take it easy, now.' She was pressed back on to the
hard surface of an examination bed with a firm but gentle

hand. 'It isn't going to help you or anybody else if you try getting on your feet and fall flat on your face, now is it? Is Adam the man who was brought in with you?'

'Adam?' Willow's mind was still hazy and she stared at the questioner in confusion for a moment.

Somewhere in the back of her mind she was aware that her prime concern should have been for Richard, yet so far she hadn't even asked after him. She could only think of Adam who had been closest to that terrifying drop when they overtook him, and the cold heavy weight in her stomach became colder; tears welling into her eyes that she could do nothing about.

'Hey now, don't let's get too uptight about this,' the white coat told her with professional cheerfulness. 'If you're so concerned about him I'll see what I can find out; is this Adam your boy-friend?'

Willow gazed at her uncertainly for a moment, biting hard on her lower lip. 'Yes—no!' She put a hand to her throbbing head and discovered bandages, exploring gingerly with her fingers while she gazed at the woman doctor with startled eyes. 'What—why am I bandaged up?' she asked, and the doctor smiled patiently and shook her head.

'You had a bang,' she explained with professional offhandedness. 'You'll be fine when you've rested a while. We'll be taking an X-ray, but there's nothing for you to worry about, it's purely routine.'

'But——' Willow screwed up her eyes, finding it frighteningly difficult to concentrate, 'how many others were brought in with me?'

'Only one casualty,' the doctor assured her, 'and he's got off pretty lightly.'

Still thinking of Adam, Willow pressed on. 'There were two cars——'

'Three, so we understand,' the doctor interrupted cheerfully, 'and according to the drivers everybody is accounted for, so I guess that includes your friend Adam, huh?' The bland, kindly face looked down at her for a moment, then a hand patted hers consolingly. 'Hey, look, there's a tall good-looking guy out there who keeps asking after you—suppose I get him in here to hold your hand for a couple of minutes, will that make you feel better?'

Richard, with a hangover and a conscience, Willow guessed ruefully, and wasn't too surprised that she didn't really want to see him. But it was a kind gesture on the doctor's part, and she didn't like to turn it down, so she nodded her head just once, jerkily. 'Yes, please,' she whispered.

'O.K. Then just you lie nice and quiet, and I'll get him.'

It was automatic to close her eyes when the doctor left her, but she opened them again when she heard the door open and turned her head hopefully, her face tearful and childishly pathetic as she stared at the man who stood just inside the room. 'I've been allowed in to see you for a few seconds,' Adam said in his soft, quiet voice, and Willow swallowed hard.

The tears started anew as she looked at him standing there, without a mark on him as far as she could see, when she had been haunted by the thought of him lying twisted and bloody at the foot of that awful drop. He was perhaps a little paler than usual and there were dark shadows circling his eyes, but that was all.

'Adam! Oh, Adam, I thought——' She tried to go on, but relief choked her, and she held out her hands to him instinctively, while tears coursed down her face, blinding her for the time it took him to walk across the room to her.

He took her hands and his strong fingers clasped them tightly, seeking to comfort her; then he held them with his left hand against his chest while the other gently smoothed the hair back from her bandaged forehead. She was crying uncontrollably, mostly with relief, but Adam wasn't to know that. 'Ssh, that's enough,' he said with pseudo-sternness. 'No one's been hurt any worse than a few bruises, except you.' The soothing fingers had a slow, almost hypnotic effect that filled her with a sudden urgent need to be in his arms. 'Poor baby,' he whispered. 'You got the worst of it, but you're not as bad as I feared you'd be, so don't cry any more. You're O.K., I promise. Please, Willow, don't cry.'

Willow needed so much to cling to him at that moment, to have him hold her tightly, and being denied the comfort of his arms she turned her face to the hardness of the hospital bed and sobbed miserably, 'I—I want to—to——'

'Willow! Oh, you poor sweet!' He leaned over her and gathered her into his arms, holding her close, with her bandaged head on his shoulder and his voice softly re-assuring against her cheek. 'Please don't cry any more or you'll make your poor head even worse.' He pressed his lips to her tear-wet face in small, light, tender kisses. 'Ssh, sweetheart, ssh!'

But Willow found relief in tears, and an answer to her emotional needs in the strength of Adam's arms; she didn't even give Richard a thought for the moment. It was several moments before she gave a great shuddering sigh and stopped crying, but she still clung to Adam because she couldn't yet bear to lose his strength. Even when he spoke her name she didn't look up.

'Willow?'

She stirred, but closed her eyes again, and her hand over his heart felt the hard, steady beat of it. 'I—I thought you'd gone—over the edge—of the road.' Her voice was husky and tears still caught at her breath between the words. 'I—I thought you would—be—hurt or——'

Adam eased her away from him slowly, and for the first time she noticed the deep, dark look in his eyes even though he smiled faintly. 'I'm sorry to disappoint you,' he teased gently. 'Is that why you're so upset? Because I didn't end up at the bottom of Copper's Drift?'

'Oh, Adam!'

'Oh, Willow!' he echoed her softly, and a glimmer of laughter showed in his eyes for a moment. Her eyes reproached him, but she wished she knew exactly why she had burst into those floods of tears the moment he walked into the room. And it did nothing to help her think more clearly when he stroked a hand slowly over her bruised cheek and smiled. 'I'm just teasing you,' he told her gently. 'But I think it's time you lay back on the bed again, sweetheart, before the doc comes and orders me out, hmm?'

Willow would much rather have stayed right where she was, even though her head ached abominably, and he was beginning to be much too free with the endearments, a prerogative that should have been Richard's. Adam lowered her carefully back on to the bed once more, and from there she looked up at him from below heavy lids. 'I should have asked,' she confessed. 'How—how is Richard?'

Immediately Adam's brows came together in a straight line, and his mouth tightened. 'He came off much better than he deserved, seeing the chance he took,' he told her with the uncompromising harshness she always hated in him. 'He should have broken his damned neck doing a damned fool thing like he did!'

'Oh no, Adam!'

He looked at her for a moment with glittering eyes, then shook his head. 'I guess you think I'm a pretty hard case, don't you, Willow?'

'I didn't say that!' she disclaimed hastily, and Adam smiled faintly.

'Well, he's getting a tough time from the police department at the moment, so he's probably wishing he *had* broken his neck.'

That was unexpected and Willow stared up at him with startled eyes. 'The—the police? The police have got him?'

'He's not in custody, if that's what you mean,' Adam told her with what she considered a callous lack of concern for his brother, whatever he had done. 'But a crash like that can't just be swept up and forgotten, Willow. The police were involved the moment it happened, and even I can't deny whose fault it was.'

'No. No, of course not.'

Her voice was small and unhappy and she felt so help-less lying there on her back with her head throbbing so much she couldn't think clearly. Yet she couldn't deny Richard's fault either, not while she could still recall the haunting horror of these few moments immediately before the crash. Of Adam's head silhouetted by the headlights, and Richard's yell of triumph as he pulled out to overtake him, and she shivered.

'Why in hell didn't he slow down when I signalled him to?' Adam asked, and she shook her head because Adam knew well enough why not. 'I tried to tell him there was another car coming, out of his line of vision, but he was so bent on putting one over on me that I guess he just wasn't thinking straight. How in God's name we all got off so lightly, I'll never know—it could have been a massacre!'

'I'm the only one hurt?'

'Richard has a few bruises and a slight cut over one eye, but that's all. You took the worst of it.' He placed a hand gently on her bandaged head and the look in his eyes was darkly sympathetic. 'But the doctor is pretty sure they won't find anything serious on the X-ray, and just one night in here under observation and you'll be out and about again.'

But Willow was far from reassured, and she stared at him. She had an almost pathological dislike of hospitals and having to stay there, even for just one night, hadn't even crossed her mind. 'Adam, I don't have to stay in surely. If the X-ray proves I'm all right, I won't have to stay in!'

'Hey, now wait a minute!' He recognised the beginning of panic in her plea, and squeezed her hands reassuringly. 'It's only for one night, so you be a sensible girl and do as they say—O.K.?'

Gentle as it was, his voice suggested that he would brook no argument, and Willow's heart beat hard and fast as she lay there looking up at him. Then the threat of tears shimmered in her eyes again. 'You *would* be on their side,' she accused plaintively, and turned her head away when she noticed him smile faintly.

'Of course,' he agreed softly. Then putting a hand either side of her on the bed he leaned over so that the lean warmth of his body touched her, and stirred those alarming reactions into being again. 'Will you promise me you'll stay until they've made quite sure you're O.K.?' he asked and, seeing herself with little option in the circumstances, Willow nodded, just once. 'Good girl!'

She wasn't sure she liked being commended in such childish terms, but there was nothing childish about the brief pressure of Adam's mouth on hers, or the momentary sensation of being pinned down to the hospital bed by his full weight. And when she looked at him again she saw that disturbing look of desire in his eyes; and it was perhaps that which prompted her to say what she did. Because it reminded her of the last time he had kissed her.

'Adam—I'm sorry I slapped you.'

Her voice was very small and husky, and Adam looked down at her steadily for a second or two. 'I'm sorry I gave you cause,' he said quietly, and bent once more to kiss her mouth. 'Goodnight, sweetheart,' he whispered, and Willow closed her eyes again.

CHAPTER SIX

'I KNOW I was lucky to get off so lightly,' said Richard, and Willow, with one hand to her throbbing head, ruefully admitted agreement.

'I still can't quite see how you managed it,' she told him. 'My memory of what happened is a bit vague, but from what I do remember it seems incredible that any of us got out of it with so little damage. I gather the driver of the other car wasn't hurt at all.'

'I suppose Adam gave you all the details last night?'

Willow recognised his resentment and knew that at least part of it was because Adam had been allowed in to see her last night and he hadn't. 'He told me that no one was seriously hurt,' she said, passing over Adam's expressed opinion of what would have happened to Richard if he had got his just deserts. 'Actually I wasn't in a very receptive mood for details, I was just thankful that you and Adam were all right.'

'Adam?' He frowned as if he found her meaning hard to follow. 'Why shouldn't he be O.K.? *He* didn't crash.'

'No thanks to you!' Willow retorted, finding it irresistible. His seeming refusal to face the seriousness of what he had done irritated her. 'We could all have been killed, Richard. As it is I'm stuck here in this wretched hospital with no chance of getting out today as I'd hoped.'

It was very quiet in the little hospital room, and she could sense his resentment. She knew just how defensive he was going to be because she had blamed him, but just as surely she knew he would appeal for her sympathy rather than fight her about it. Richard was made that way. He sat beside her bed, holding her hands, and she tried to stop herself feeling sorry for him. Only minutes before he arrived she had been informed by one of the doctors that it would be better if she stayed in hospital for at least another few days, and it had been Richard's foolhardiness that put her in there. She didn't feel like being sympathetic.

He sat with his head bowed and looked quite incredibly contrite, and his sigh seemed to come from the heart. 'O.K., have your say,' he told her. 'I guess I have it coming.'

Because she felt rather guilty about suddenly wanting to giggle hysterically, Willow reached and touched his hand. 'I'm sorry,' she told him in a resigned kind of voice. 'I can't say that you weren't at fault, but I wouldn't have nagged you if I wasn't feeling so grotty. My head still aches despite all the pills they've been giving me, and knowing I have to stay in this place for heaven knows how much longer doesn't help.' His face looked so woebegone that she shook her head. 'Look, suppose *you* tell me exactly what happened last night, and I'll try not to go to sleep while you're talking.'

It took Richard no time at all to realise he had won her round, and when he looked at her and smiled, Willow thought that, even bruised and battered as he was, he was still devastatingly attractive. His good-looking face was decorated with a long strip of sticking plaster over one eye, and there was a dark, puffy bruise under the same eye.

Another bruise, even blacker, showed along the length of his jaw, but instead of detracting from his looks, the whole effect of rather piratical boldness seemed to add something. Something that had been quite enough to put a sparkle into the eyes of the stout blonde nurse who had admitted him, and it occurred to Willow that Richard would never be short of women admirers, even if she wasn't around herself.

His confidence restored, he squeezed her fingers and pressed them briefly to his lips. 'Did Adam tell you about the other car that was coming around the bend?' he asked, and she nodded. 'He says that's why he was trying to slow me down, only how was I to know? On Copper's Drift, at that time of night——'

'It was unlucky,' Willow allowed, but her tone made it clear that she didn't exonerate him, even so, and he shook his head slowly, squeezing the hand he held.

'The thing I'm most sorry about is you being in here,' he said. 'I feel bad about it, Willow, and I wish there was something I could do to make it up to you. Adam has offered to crack me over the skull so that I know what it feels like, but I didn't think you'd want me to go that far, however sorry I am.'

'Did he really say that?' Willow couldn't resist a faint smile, and it gave her a curious kind of satisfaction to know that Adam felt so strongly about her being hurt. 'Never mind, Richard, I don't think *he'd* go that far, whatever he says.'

'You don't know him,' Richard told her with un-expected solemnity. 'He's got a savage streak that would surprise you, and he's real mad at me over this. He wouldn't even let me drive in to see you this morning; he turned me down flat when I asked to borrow his car, and I had to take a cab.'

That wasn't unexpected, although Willow didn't say so. 'Is your own car very badly damaged?' she asked.

'Pretty bad. It'll be some time before I get it back, although I have a sneaky hunch that Adam has bribed Sam Portera to keep it longer than he need!'

'Oh, Richard, he wouldn't! What would be the point?'

'To keep me off the road,' Richard answered promptly, and even as he said it Willow realised that Adam would be perfectly capable of doing as he said.

'How about asking your grandmother?' she suggested. 'She very seldom goes out in her car.'

'She seldom goes against Adam either,' Richard told her ruefully. 'I'm never her favourite species and I'm really in dutch now I've endangered the life and limb of her favourite grandson No—I guess I may as well resign myself to using cabs for a while yet.'

In spite of everything, it was impossible not to feel some sympathy for him, although Willow found something vaguely comical about his self-pity which she did her best not to let him see. 'Poor Richard,' she murmured. 'You really have made a hash of things, haven't you?'

Turning her hand over, he laid his bruised cheek against her palm and looked at her appealingly. 'I really don't deserve your sympathy,' he said, 'but I'm grateful for it just the same. I shouldn't have tried to pass on that road, and I shouldn't have been driving in the state I was in. Much as I hate to admit it, Adam was right—I was too sloshed to be safe.'

'We both were,' Willow told him consolingly, but

having found the way to win her sympathy Richard shook his head firmly.

'*I* was driving,' he insisted, 'and it was sheer luck that there was room for the guy in the other car to pull over at that point, otherwise we'd all have gone over. I just wish it could have been me who got tossed out and not you, sweetheart.'

'Not if you had my head, you wouldn't,' Willow told him ruefully. 'And what good would it have done?'

'Well, it would have given Adam more satisfaction, for one thing,' Richard assured her gloomily. 'Right now he's treating me like some kind of dangerous nut who should be locked up, and the opinion seems to be pretty general if you ask me. Even that dishy lady doc last night let him in to see you because she took one look at me with the cops round my neck and figured I wasn't a fit person to be talking to her patient.'

'Oh, what nonsense!'

Whenever he was on the defensive, Willow noticed, he spattered his speech with slang, and she found it vaguely amusing, despite her aching head, but Richard was deadly serious. 'Then how come he got in and I couldn't?' he demanded. 'I'm your fiancé, but *he* gets in to see you!'

'He'd been asking to see me,' Willow ventured, and Richard glared.

'You think I hadn't?' he demanded indignantly, and she shook her head, preferring not to meet his eyes suddenly.

Adam's brief visit last night was something she would rather not talk about, and particularly not to Richard. It seemed there had been too many episodes lately that she had thought best to keep from Richard, all of them involving Adam in one way or another. All in all she wasn't sure how much longer she could go on pretending that she saw Adam as no more or less than Richard's brother.

Using her free hand in a touchingly appealing gesture, she looked up at him from the pillows and wished her head didn't throb so persistently. 'I'm sorry, Richard,' she told him, 'but I honestly didn't expect to see Adam when the doctor said she would allow me a few minutes' visit.'

'But you didn't send him away!'

How could she have? Willow thought. She had been so unutterably relieved to see him unharmed. 'I was just glad to see a familiar face,' she said, and Richard held her hand almost painfully tight for a moment before bursting out furiously.

'Oh, damn it—why couldn't Adam have got tight and slung his girl out on her head!' Then seeing her expression, he laughed a little shamefacedly and kissed her fingers. 'One thing's for sure, baby—if he had, Marsha Sai-Hung wouldn't have looked half so good with her head bandaged and two black eyes.'

'Black eyes?' Willow stared at him in dismay and for the moment everything else was forgotten. 'Oh, Richard, I haven't, have I?'

'Well,' Richard said, his eyes teasing, 'more a cute shade of purple, I guess.' He laughed at her look of dismay, then got up from his chair and sat on the side of the bed instead. 'I'm only teasing, sweetheart. You have a couple of bruises on your cheeks, that's all, and they aren't as dark as mine, don't worry. And what I said still goes; Marsha wouldn't look near so good, I swear it.'

Willow's head was aching and the last person she wanted to hear mentioned was Marsha Sai-Hung. She half wished Richard would go and leave her to sleep off the tablets she had been given. 'I don't suppose Adam would think any less of her, however she looked,' she observed with a touch of acid, and Richard shrugged.

'I guess not,' he conceded. 'She's his type, like you're mine.'

'Is she?' Willow lay with a hand pressed to her forehead and her eyes half closed, irritable suddenly without quite knowing why. 'I was under the impression that opposites attract, in which case Adam should prefer something a little more—soft—and feminine.'

Richard said nothing for a moment, but she was aware of him watching her steadily, even though her eyes were closed, and she opened them again swiftly when he leaned over her. 'So you've got it all figured out, eh?'

Frowning slightly because she found it hard to concentrate on anything at the moment, Willow scarcely bothered to answer him. 'It's not that important,' she said faintly.

He remained where he was, looking down at her, but she was finding it increasingly hard to keep awake. 'You look as if you need a rest, sweetheart,' he said softly. 'They told me not to stay too long and tire you, so I'd better go.' He leaned closer suddenly, placing a hand either side of her on the pillows, just as Adam had last night, and when she looked up Willow noticed that his eyes were narrowed slightly and there was an unfamiliar shrewdness in their depths. Then he bent and kissed her before hovering again, holding her reluctant gaze. 'If by soft and feminine you're thinking of somebody like you, my darling,' he murmured, 'no way!'

He bent and kissed her again, a hard firm kiss, then he was gone, and she had barely time to turn her head and see the door close behind him.

Willow had been four nights and nearly four days in hospital, and she was anxious to leave before someone decided she ought to stay longer. Not that she hadn't been very well treated—the power and wealth of the le Bruns had its advantages—but she had such an aversion to hospitals that she couldn't wait to leave.

The moment she had been given the word, she had made a hasty telephone call to La Bonne Terre and Madame le Brun had promised that they would be delighted to have her back, and that someone would certainly call and fetch her and bring more clothes for her. Although she hadn't actually spoken to Richard, Willow felt sure he would be coming to take her home, and her stomach churned excitedly as she got herself ready.

The nurse who brought her case in helped her into the dress that Madame le Brun had sent, chattering happily as she hovered around, friendly and encouraging. 'Hey you must have something very special, honey,' she told Willow archly, and surveyed her sleeveless green dress and the figure it revealed with goodhumoured envy. 'All these good-looking guys turning up for you! I guess it must be that red hair and green eyes, huh?'

Willow looked at her curiously. The woman knew what Richard looked like, for he had flirted with her outrageously each time he came visiting, and made her giggle like a schoolgirl. 'Surely Mr Richard le Brun has come for me, hasn't he?' she asked, a small niggle of suspicion in the back of her mind.

'Is he the one who came before?' the nurse asked. She was middle-aged and stocky and unashamedly fond of the opposite sex, and she chuckled happily when Willow nodded her head. 'Then it ain't him, honey. This one's older, but just as dishy; you sure have the luck!'

Suddenly Willow was much more nervous, knowing that Adam was waiting out there for her, and she smoothed down her dress and put a tentative hand to the plaster that now decorated her forehead in place of the bandage. It was idiotic to feel as she did, but it was all too easy to recall the warm pressure of Adam's body as she lay on the hospital bed, and the gentle but sensual touch of his mouth, and she shivered.

'You O.K.?' the nurse asked, and she nodded. The woman showed her where Adam was waiting and gave her a broad wink as she handed over her suitcase. 'See what I mean?' she said. 'Bye, honey, have a nice day!'

The reception area was so crowded that it seemed to make anything but a formal greeting out of the question. Nevertheless Adam's grey eyes studied her closely for a moment, noting among other things the bright colour in her cheeks. 'Shall we go?' he asked, and slipped a hand under her arm—a service she accepted gladly, since her legs were alarmingly unsteady.

It was the first time she had seen him since the night of the crash and it gave Willow a curiously exciting feeling to be going home with him, even though he was so quiet. So far he hadn't even asked how she was feeling, but possibly he was waiting until they left the clinical impersonality of the hospital, and her guess seemed to be confirmed when he turned to her the moment they emerged from the swing doors and into the open air.

'Are you sure you're feeling O.K.?' he asked, and Willow smiled.

'I'm feeling fine now that I'm out of that place,' she assured him. 'My legs feel a bit unsteady after all that time in bed and just shuffling around the ward, but I'm so glad to be out I feel like dancing!'

He half smiled, mocking her enthusiasm, she suspected. 'Did they treat you well?'

'Very well,' she said. 'But I just don't like hospitals and I was so afraid somebody was coming to say I had to stay longer, before you came for me.'

His hand still supported her as they crossed the car park, and just briefly his long cool fingers pressed into her flesh. 'I guess you don't always know what's best for you,' he remarked. 'You were slightly concussed, and rest and quiet are the prescribed cure.'

'Oh yes, I know, but I have a real fear of those places— I don't know why.'

She glanced at him and saw that he was smiling faintly. 'You're an odd little creature,' he mused, and something about the way he said it seemed to consign her to the infant class, so that she flushed and looked at him indignantly.

'That may be your opinion,' she retorted, 'but it isn't everyone's!'

They were standing beside his car and the sun seemed so incredibly hot that she felt a sudden brief return of the pain in her head. His fingers pressed into her flesh again for a moment and he narrowed his eyes slightly against the sun as he looked down at her. 'It wasn't a criticism,' he said in that stunningly affecting voice of his. 'You're a very lovely girl, even with——'

'If you say two black eyes I shall scream!' Willow warned swiftly, and to her chagrin he laughed.

'I was going to say with a plaster across your forehead,' he told her, 'but it does look as if you've had two black eyes at that.' He bent and peered close at her face for a second and the whisping warmth of his breath teased her mouth. 'Did it dent your feminine pride, having a black eye, Willow?'

'I didn't *have* a black eye,' she denied firmly. 'It was just Richard being funny! I—I had bruises on my cheeks—you saw them.'

'So I did.' He spoke softly, and the tone of his voice reminded her of when he had bent over her as she lay on the bed, and the touch of his mouth on hers. She almost jumped out of her skin when he ran his fingertips, very lightly, down her flushed cheeks. 'Well, you're not bruised now, you're as pink and white and beautiful as you ever were, hmm?'

She had taken no notice when he leaned past her to open the car door, but the sudden light pressure of his mouth was unexpected and she caught her breath, wary as she so often was with him. He said nothing as he saw her into her seat, but there was a curiously enigmatic smile on his face as he closed the door on her and it made her distinctly uneasy.

'Let's get you home,' he said softly, and Willow felt her heart give a sudden violent lurch when he slid into the driving seat beside her a moment later, for the light, brief touch of his body took her by surprise. If only she could do something about her unfailing response to him it would make things so much easier.

'I—I didn't expect you,' she ventured as they drove out of the car park, and Adam gave her a brief smile, faintly speculative.

'You thought Richard would come for you?' he asked. 'Well—yes.'

'I guess he would have, but he doesn't have a car,' Adam reminded her quietly. 'And you didn't want to come home in a cab, did you?'

He made it all sound so matter-of-fact, and yet Willow couldn't imagine that Richard had simply yielded up his right to fetch her as easily as that. 'I—I don't know. I suppose not. But I thought Richard would have come.'

He gave his attention to the traffic on the main highway for a while, then he half turned his head. 'Sorry to disappoint you,' he said, and said no more for the moment.

Willow sat with her hands in her lap and her arms drawn in close to her sides in an attempt to avoid any further contact with bare brown arms, and heaven knew what made her look for the small pulse she had noticed on other occasions. She had noticed it beating steadily at the base of his throat, but it seemed now to be beating harder and faster than it ever had before, and seeing it made her own heart beat a little faster without any discernible reason.

As they sped along between the wide open pineapple fields, Adam turned his head again suddenly. 'Did Richard tell you that the police are likely to come down heavily on him for drunken driving?'

Willow shook her head, though she couldn't claim to be surprised by it. 'Poor Richard,' she said, automatically, and Adam turned his head sharply again and frowned.

'Poor Richard?' he echoed with heavy sarcasm. 'Don't you realise that he could have killed four people that night, including himself? Don't go feeling too sorry for him, Willow, he deserves everything he's going to get, and with a bit of luck it will teach him to behave like an adult!'

'I know, I know!' She looked at him reproachfully. 'But you don't have to crow over him quite so—so gloatingly, surely! It could have happened to anyone. Even you,' she added with deliberate malice, and his short bark of laughter startled her.

'Well, you stick by him, I'll say that for you,' he told

her, with obviously grudging admiration, 'even if your loyalty is misplaced. But you're wrong if you think it could happen to me, Willow. I'd never take chances like Richard did with my own life, let alone with the girl I professed to love.'

'I'm sure Mrs Sai-Hung would be very relieved to hear it!' she retorted swiftly, then wondered why on earth she had been so rash as to make a remark like that at this particular moment.

'Marsha?' His voice had a softness that made her skin prickle, and she looked at him uneasily from the corner of her eye. 'What has Marsha Sai-Hung to do with what we were talking about?'

Willow moistened her lips anxiously, glancing every so often at Adam's stern profile turned so discouragingly to her. 'You know what I mean,' she accused. 'You and— Richard says——'

'Ah yes,' Adam interrupted softly. 'We've been through this before, haven't we? Richard thinks I'm destined to be Marsha's number two, isn't that what you said?' Willow didn't reply, she didn't even nod her head, and he glanced at her again briefly. 'You figure we'll make a good pair, Willow?'

The challenge was not only unexpected but impossible to answer, and she shook her head; warily, because it was aching again. 'How—how do I know?' she whispered at last, and Adam's voice almost cut across her words.

'How indeed?' he asked silkily, then was silent again for a moment. 'You don't like her, do you?'

It wasn't really a question but more of a statement, and Willow didn't bother to deny it. 'You can hardly be surprised,' she said, 'after what she did to me.'

He darted her a swift glance from the corner of his eye, then gave his attention to turning off the main highway and on to the smaller road that led to La Bonne Terre, but there was a certain air about him that made her suspect he read something more into her reply than she intended. The moment they were on the smaller road, he pulled in to the side and braked the car to a halt, half turning in his seat to look at her for a moment before he said anything, while Willow coped with yet another violent lurch in her heartbeat.

'You're talking about that day you—went swimming?' he asked quietly, and the way he used one hand to convey his meaning brought a flush to her cheeks again. 'I know what she did was unforgivable, it was criminally dangerous if you want to be honest about it, but Marsha is a very passionate woman and she acts without thinking— passionate in more ways than one,' he added with a faint lift of one dark brow. He slid a hand under her chin and turned her to face him, studying her for a moment before he went on. 'But there's something more than that, isn't there, Willow?' he insisted softly. 'Have there been other times, other—incidents?'

Willow would much rather not have said anything more on the subject of Marsha Sai-Hung, but she knew it was no use denying there wasn't anything else. Not to Adam— she knew him better than that. 'Only one,' she told him reluctantly. 'The night of the Kimuraz' party——'

Adam was swearing softly under his breath and the brief glimpse she allowed herself of his face, she noticed how his eyes burned fiercely. 'You fell into the fountain,' he said. 'Only you didn't *fall* in, did you, Willow?'

She shook her head, finding no satisfaction at all in telling him. 'I—I thought it was best.'

'Why, in heaven's name?' His fingers were light and gentle on her cheeks and the touch of him was as affecting as ever, so that she half closed her eyes and kept them downcast.

His grey eyes remained fixed on her flushed and uncertain face, and he must have known how unwillingly she admitted the truth, yet he still pressed on. All too often lately there had been incidents that she told herself she would rather had not happened. But when she thought of Adam's arms around her and Adam's mouth on hers, she knew she didn't really regret a single moment of those deliriously exciting moments, no matter what Marsha Sai-Hung did, or how guilty it made her feel about Richard.

'Why?' he insisted, and his voice shivered along her spine like a caressing finger. 'It would have made much more sense if you'd let everyone know what she'd done and let her take the consequences. Why didn't you?'

It wasn't exactly the reaction she expected of him, and she said nothing for a moment. It wasn't easy to explain to him, and she nervously moistened her lips before she attempted to tell him. 'I—I suppose I felt that she had—some kind of excuse,' she said, and from the sound he made Adam understood her meaning but did not necessarily agree with it.

'What possible excuse could she have for behaving like that?'

Again Willow flicked her tongue over her lips and shook her head, for it was becoming increasingly hard to put her feelings into words. 'I—thought at first that she knew—I'd just left you——'

'I remember,' Adam said quietly, and just briefly she glanced up at him. 'You thought she knew I'd been with you—just kissed you,' he went on, still in the same quiet, almost matter-of-fact voice, and Willow nodded.

'But I'm pretty sure she didn't,' she told him. 'She just kept on about me—about you seeing me in that pool below the crater; she's sure I was—she thinks I did it deliberately because I knew you were there, and you know it isn't true, Adam, you know I wouldn't have——'

A light brush with his lips silenced her, and he cradled her face between his big hands for a moment looking down at her lowered eyes and the bright warm flush in her cheeks. 'I know you wouldn't have,' he said softly, 'and I'm sorry it happened as it did, Willow, but I had no idea that Marsha was about.'

'You think it would have made a difference to how I felt about you being there?' Willow demanded, then shook her head, freeing herself from those caressing hands. 'Oh, it was my own fault for being so—so stupid, but I just didn't think anyone would see me up there.'

'Nor would they have, if I hadn't been concerned about you getting lost or hurting yourself in unfamiliar territory,' Adam insisted quietly. There was something in his voice that sent little shivers all along her spine, and she dared not look up at him for the moment, although she almost did when he once more cupped his hands around her face and tilted it up to him. 'But I'm not going to say I'm sorry I followed you, Willow.' The words fluttered warmly against her lips, and she actually shivered.

'Adam, please don't——'

He sighed as if he saw no reason for her high colour, or the evasive eyes that refused to meet his, but something told her that he did not regret having seen her, only that she was embarrassed about it. Adam was a frankly sensual man and he saw no reason to disguise his pleasure in her feminine nakedness.

'I'd be grateful if you'd just forget it ever happened,' she told him, and glanced up in sudden alarm when she realised he was shaking his head.

'I can't promise to forget it, Willow,' he murmured in that deep and infinitely disturbing voice, 'but I will promise that nobody'll hear about it from me.'

'And Mrs Sai-Hung?'

He heaved his broad shoulders in a gesture of helplessness. 'I can't answer for Marsha,' he admitted frankly. 'But I can't see that it would do her any good to tell anybody, can you?'

Willow followed his meaning and nodded—then immediately regretted it when a brief thud of pain ran through her head, and she put a hand to her forehead. Adam edged towards her slightly, looking anxious, and she hastened to reassure him. 'My head aches a bit,' she told him with a ghost of a smile. 'I never remember not to nod or shake my head.'

'Poor baby!'

When he stroked his fingers down her cheeks and brushed back the hair from her brow it was all too reminiscent of the night of the accident, and she caught her breath at the responsive flutter of her heart. His hand lingered, light and sensual on her neck, and when he lifted her chin it was instinctive to look up at him, her lips parted and moistened by the swift flick of her tongue.

'Richard has a lot to answer for,' he said. 'He could have killed you.'

'And himself,' she reminded him. 'It was mad to drive in the state he was in, but he admits it and he's sorry, and I believe him.'

'Forgive and forget, eh?' Adam suggested, and something in his voice brought fresh colour to her cheeks. Then he sighed. 'Oh, Willow, how I wish you'd give him up before you really get hurt.'

Again the suggestion came as a surprise, and once more she reacted impulsively. Heedless of the niggling ache in her head, she jerked herself free of those gentle hands and leaned back, looking at him with reproachful green eyes and utterly confused by her own emotions. 'Still on that same theme!' she sighed. 'Don't you ever give up, Adam? You want Richard in your wretched company and you think by getting me to leave him you'll find it easier to—to pressure him! Why bother with all this so-called concern for me? Why should you care if I get hurt as long as you get Richard into the company?'

'Of course I care, you little idiot!' He gripped her upper arms in his hands and turned her to face him again. 'You think it's just because of the company that I'm trying to break up this thing with Richard? Now I know you better, I know I don't even have a fight on my hands, but I can't stand to see somebody like you being used as Richard's using you. And you just won't see it, will you?'

'Because it isn't true!'

It made her uneasy to remember Richard's evasiveness whenever marriage was mentioned, but she hastily dismissed the possibility of there being anything very significant in that, and shook her head. Her own naked left hand seemed to spring to notice when she glanced down

at it, but again she dismissed any possible significance. A
ring wasn't essential, as she had been ready to agree in
the first place; although occasionally since—

It was a mistake to have looked at Adam when she was
feeling as she did at that moment, for the impatience in
his eyes was merged with another and much more alarming expression. Recognising that fierce, almost savage look
of desire was her undoing, for her senses responded as
they always did, and everything seemed to happen so
quickly.

Adam bound her close with the strength of his arms
and pressed her against the soft leather seat with the
weight of his body, bringing his face close enough to warm
her lips with his breath. She vaguely murmured some kind
of protest, but it was smothered almost at once by a mouth
that took hers with all the fierceness she had come to
expect of him, and she clung to him as she had done
before, because it seemed the only thing she could do.

His hands moving over her back were strong and per-
suasive, stroking up over her shoulders and pushing down
the thin cotton dress until the front fastening gave way,
and he pressed his lips to her throat and the soft, urgent
swell of her breasts. Her fingers tangled in thick red-brown
hair, she held his head in her hands, her arms lifted to
rest on the side of his neck, and at that moment Richard
had never been further from her mind.

His mouth was buried in the softness of her neck, in the
pulsing hollow between neck and shoulder, and as he
murmured softly Willow turned her face and touched her
lips to the tanned warmth of his throat, seeking the tiny
pulse that now beat urgently at its base. It was minutes
before he raised his head and looked down at her for a
moment with eyes that still burned with such passion she
shivered.

'Give him up,' he whispered huskily. 'In God's name,
you can't love him—give him up before it's too late!'

It struck Willow like a blow, for her first thought was
that persuasion was Adam's reason for kissing her like

that, and she pushed with her hands on his chest, her eyes
hot with anger because he had fooled her. She recalled
how he had kissed her that first time, very shortly after
she arrived. At least in that instance he had been honest
about his motives, but never since, except for that night
at the party, when he had sought the same end.

Twisting round straight in her seat, she sat with her
hands tightly clasped together and her cheeks burning. 'I
just never learn, do I?' she said in a voice that trembled
in spite of her efforts, and her laughter was a poor apology
for humour. 'You'll try anything to make me give up
Richard, and I never realise until it's too late that you're
making a fool of me.'

'Willow, in God's name——'

'In le Brun's name, surely,' Willow interrupted. 'That's
what concerns you, isn't it, Adam? Richard is a le Brun
and he must conform, regardless of what he wants to do,
and you think that the only way to get him into line is to
get rid of me!' Adam said nothing, but the look in his eyes
sent little shivers scuttling along her back. 'You're wrong,
but you'll never admit to being wrong, will you? And
you'll do anything—*anything*,' she stressed bitterly, 'to
make things happen your way! How you have the nerve
to suggest that Richard's using me——!'

His silence was almost more ominous than an outburst
of anger would have been, and she could feel his eyes on
her for a full minute after she finished her tirade. Then he
turned without a word and started the engine, slamming
the car into motion so quickly that she was thrown forward in her seat and put out a hand to stop herself.

Once, just briefly, as they neared the house Adam half
turned his head as if he would have said something, then
abruptly changed his mind. But in the second that he
looked at her Willow thought she saw that look of gentleness in his eyes again and clasped her hands more tightly
against succumbing to temptation. But it was too much
not to take a swift sideways glance at him as he drove her
back to La Bonne Terre and Richard.

'I was hoping to come and fetch you myself,' Richard told her that same evening after dinner, 'but with one thing and the other Grand'mère figured it was better if Adam came. You know how it is.'

'I can guess,' Willow told him, 'but *I* wish you'd come for me too.'

Something in her voice caught his attention and he frowned at her curiously. 'Was it as bad as that?' he asked. 'I thought he looked a bit grim when he set out, but we've all been worried about you. You're still a bit— wary of him, aren't you?' he added as if her reasons puzzled him.

She would be even more wary after today, Willow thought, but she could not say as much to Richard. 'I suppose I am,' she admitted. 'I'm never quite sure which category he puts me in—just straightforward fiancée or a nasty little gold-digger after the le Brun dollars.'

Richard, as usual, didn't take it seriously, and he laughed as he bent to kiss her cheek. 'He should know the trouble I had getting you to come here with me! If you'd been after the le Brun dollars you'd have jumped at the chance to come, not had to be persuaded.'

Willow looked up at him and smiled faintly. 'But maybe Adam sees me as more devious than you do.' Firmly dismissing the subject of Adam, she smiled more brightly. 'Have you kept up your practising while I've been away?' she asked, and frowned at him curiously when he didn't reply at once, but sat with his hands clasped together between his knees, looking thoughtful.

'I haven't done any, in fact.'

Not quite sure what to say, Willow smiled. 'Lack of inspiration?'

He shrugged, and something about his manner made her suddenly suspicious. 'I guess you could say that.' They were sitting together on one of the garden seats and he raised one of her hands and pressed the palm to his cheek. 'According to Adam I've seen the light, and I guess he's right as usual.'

'Seen the light?'

Richard nodded. Quite clearly he wasn't at ease, and there was a suggestion of bravado in his smile. 'I met Adam half way. I've been to the office with him a couple of times this past week, just to see what it's like.'

'I see.'

Willow felt oddly chilled suddenly, for he had just confirmed what she had accused Adam of. She had been away only four days, but in that time he had talked Richard into doing as he wanted; with her permanently out of the way he would have little trouble keeping him in line. And he hadn't said a word about it on the way home; that hurt too, although she would never have admitted it.

'Sweetheart,' said Richard, watching her anxiously, 'I know you maybe think I'm a creep for giving in, but— well, you know how it is.'

'I know how it is,' Willow agreed quietly. 'You've now confirmed Adam's suspicion that once I'm out of the way you'll come to heel.'

He looked more sheepish than she would have believed possible, and she felt a sudden surge of impatience for his weakness. It didn't matter to her that he wasn't going to be a musician after all, but she would have felt more satisfaction if he had at least had the strength of will to hold out for what he wanted, instead of giving in the moment she wasn't there to back him up.

'It doesn't really matter,' he told her, seemingly intent on converting her to Adam's way of thinking now that he had yielded. 'I know you rather fancied having a musician boy-friend, but—well, I'm sorry.'

'Oh, for heaven's sake, Richard!' she told him in a burst of impatience. 'It makes no difference to me one way or the other, but you were so keen to go on with your music, and now you've simply—capitulated, just as Adam guessed you would! Just as he planned you would,' she added bitterly.

'He didn't twist my arm,' Richard declared somewhat uneasily, and Willow looked at him disbelievingly. 'That's

God's truth, baby,' he insisted. 'I made my own decision to take a look at big business and see how it grabbed me.'

'Why?' She still resolutely refused to believe that the change of attitude was of his own choosing, and his expression seemed to confirm it.

He shrugged, looking down at the hand he held. 'I figured it couldn't do any harm to meet him half-way, and I was—well, I was feeling kind of guilty about you. I couldn't expect you to live like a groupie, like Adam said.'

'Oh, I see.' She nodded understanding at last. 'So he didn't bully you into it, he played on your conscience instead.'

'Hell, no, Willow!' He denied it, but Willow was convinced that something of the sort must have happened. 'You won't mention it to him, will you, sweetheart?'

'Why should I?' she asked dryly. 'It's your life, after all; hasn't that been the argument all along? That you should please yourself?'

He looked uneasy, as well he might, Willow thought. 'It'll be O.K., sweetheart. I don't have to give up the guitar altogether, I can still play.'

'So——' Willow sat upright on the bench seat and put her hands together. 'Now that you've sorted yourself out you don't really need my backing any more, do you?' Richard stared at her for a moment, and she felt a brief qualm of conscience. 'Now that *would* please Adam, if I were to go home right now.'

'Sweetheart! What are you saying?' He gripped both her hands anxiously, watching her face for some sign that she was teasing him. But Willow wasn't teasing, she felt rather lost suddenly, and she went willingly enough when Richard drew her into his arms. 'You can't leave, sweetheart, you belong here with me.'

'How long for?' Richard was looking at her curiously and Willow knew that it was only her own special knowledge of the situation that made her question the possibility of staying on in the family home. 'Even after we're married?'

He was silent for so long that Willow clenched her hands, recognising that now familiar reluctance to discuss their wedding. 'Sure, after we're married,' he said at last, in a quiet voice that reminded her of Adam. 'Why not?'

Why not indeed? Willow thought ruefully. Except that she couldn't imagine a situation more fraught with danger than living at La Bonne Terre as Richard's wife and with Adam always in close proximity. He could too easily disturb her; too easily lure her into forgetting Richard's very existence, and the thought of spending the rest of her life with that temptation always at hand didn't bear thinking about.

Lifting her head, she looked steadily at the top button on Richard's shirt while she spoke. 'I couldn't do that, Richard,' she told him quietly, and saw the quick way he frowned.

'Why not, you like it here, don't you?'

'Yes. Yes, I like it here.' She desperately sought for the right words, knowing that whatever happened she couldn't change her mind about this particular question. 'But it simply wouldn't work with all of us living together, Richard, and I think you'll find Adam agrees with me about this at least.'

'But he wants me here,' Richard insisted, 'and if he has me, he has you. Oh, you're talking crazy, sweetheart, if you think he wouldn't want you here—of course he does.'

'Richard——'

He kissed her firmly on her mouth, stemming any further argument before it was formed. 'No more nonsense,' he ordered. 'You're doing old Adam less than justice if you think he'd want us out of the old place. I think it's time you two got together and got to know one another. You never know you might get to like each other!'

He laughed, as if the idea of them not getting along was a joke, but Willow didn't find it amusing. 'We might,' she said with a catch in her voice, and hoped Richard wouldn't notice.

CHAPTER SEVEN

It was more than a week since Willow had left the hospital, and the whole tempo of her life seemed to have changed. She saw Adam no more and no less often than she always had, but he treated her very much more formally than ever before; something she regretted more than she cared to admit. On the other hand she saw a lot less of Richard because of his involvement with the company, and she had to allow for him being absent each day until lunchtime.

It was because of the new arrangements that she spent much more time with Madame le Brun, and got to know her better. She missed Richard, she had to admit, but she got along well with his grandmother, and she quite enjoyed the quiet life. The difference was that she sometimes got the feeling that the le Brun family had become a unit again, and she was an interloper.

Several times during the past week she had thought of suggesting to Richard that now he was more fully occupied she could return home, but for some reason she kept putting it off. It could be, she recognised uneasily, because she feared he might not be quite so adamantly against her going home as he had once been, and deep in her heart she didn't really want to go, despite everything.

Although she was nothing like the traditional cosy granny figure, Madame le Brun was a bright intelligent woman with an alertness that denied her years, and Willow realised she was becoming quite fond of her. She had sensed the sharp old eyes watching her for some time, and it was inevitable that sooner or later she would look up from the flowers she was arranging and smile.

'How's that?' she asked, standing aside so that her efforts could be judged, and Madame le Brun nodded.

'Not bad at all,' she told her, and that was praise indeed coming from that quarter. Then she added a totally un-expected comment that made Willow look at her uneasily, especially in view of her recent thoughts. 'You fit in very well here.'

'Do I?'

Willow's smile seemed to treat the opinion lightly, but Madame le Brun was obviously serious about it. 'You've been a pleasant surprise to me, girl.'

She invariably addressed Willow simply as 'girl', and it annoyed Richard because he swore that she did it only to keep Willow, and indirectly him, in her place. Willow, however, found it rather quaintly old-fashioned and didn't mind it in the least. 'That's nice,' she said. 'I'm very glad, *madame*.'

'You're a very sensible young woman,' Madame le Brun went on, unaware of causing any embarrassment, 'and you're a *womanly* woman. They're a little thin on the ground now, but men still prefer them, as I'm sure you're clever enough to know.'

'I don't know about that,' Willow chose another vase and gathered up a bunch of roses from the pile on the table, not knowing quite how to react. 'I've never given it much thought,' she confessed. 'As far as I know I'm like most women of my age. Isn't every woman—womanly?'

'You know what I mean, girl,' Madame le Brun told her briskly. 'You're what? Twenty-two? Twenty-three?'

'Twenty-three, *madame*.'

The old lady nodded. 'You're a little young, perhaps, but you carry yourself well, and you have a way with men that doesn't suggest you're trying to get the better of them. Even the way you arrange those flowers is feminine and leisurely. You have none of the hideous pseudo-mas-culinity that so many of your contemporaries affect.'

Willow looked up and smiled. 'I don't know that my parents would agree with you there, Madame le Brun—

at home I was considered a tomboy. Having three brothers it was inevitable, I suppose.'

'It also means you were cosseted, I dare say,' the old lady told her knowledgably, 'and that's good for any woman's femininity.' Women's Lib was a favourite hobby-horse of hers, and Willow wasn't sure whether to encourage her or not at the moment. She shortened the stem of one of the roses and held it to her nose for a moment while Madame le Brun sat watching her. 'I'm glad, for Adam's sake,' she observed, and Willow almost dropped the bloom back on to the table.

'*Adam*?' she echoed, and stared at her for a moment while her heart thudded wildly.

Madame le Brun smiled, but there was a kind of malicious mischief gleaming in her eyes that made Willow uneasy. 'I mean Richard, of course,' she amended, making it clear that the mistake had been no slip of the tongue.

Willow turned back to her flower-arranging, hoping to hide the faint colour in her cheeks. It was just possible, she supposed, that the old lady suspected the present formality between her and Adam, but she surely couldn't *know* anything. 'When is the wedding to be?' she asked, and Willow's hand tightened on the stem she held.

'We haven't fixed a definite date yet, *madame*,' she told her, and Madame le Brun gave a snort of impatience.

'That's what you always say!' she said tartly. 'It's time you set a definite date so that folks know what they're doing. Have you invited your family over yet?'

Willow shook her head. 'I've mentioned that the wedding is to be over here and not at home, but that's as far as it's got yet.'

'Your parents must be thinking the worst,' Madame le Brun observed bluntly. 'Don't you and Richard even *talk* about it?'

Driven by sheer desperation to take a chance, Willow said the first thing that came into her head. 'We thought this coming autumn,' she said, and wondered what Richard was going to say about that when he knew.

'Not till fall?' Thin brows expressed Madame's dissatisfaction. 'It's not even the middle of summer yet – that grandson of mine isn't exactly an eager lover, is he?'

'I don't think he's all that eager to be a husband,' Willow told her, skirting around Richard's eagerness to be a lover. 'But he has a lot to cope with at the moment, *madame*, and there's really no hurry.'

'He's a young fool!' his grandmother declared forcefully. 'And if he doesn't soon make a move he's going to lose out!'

It was automatic when Willow came to his defence, for she always had. 'Richard isn't a fool, Madame le Brun,' she said quietly. 'He may not see eye to eye with Adam on everything, but he isn't a fool.'

'He is if he keeps a girl like you hanging around too long,' his grandmother retorted, and her sharp eyes watched Willow push another rose into the vase. 'I guess he's finally given up the idea of being a guitarist, is that so?'

Willow nodded, somewhat reluctantly. 'It seems like it, for the time being,' she agreed.

'No stamina!' the old lady declared, and Willow swung around to face her.

'Oh, that isn't fair at all,' she protested. 'You always wanted him to join the company, you and Adam.'

'But I'd have more respect for him if he'd stuck to his music and told us to go to——' An eloquent hand finished the sentence. 'Adam would have in his place.'

Willow knew it, but it seemed very unfair just the same. 'Poor Richard,' she mourned. 'He doesn't seem able to please you one way or the other. If he wants to go his own way he's a fool, and if he does as you want him to he's a fool—he can't win!'

'He's a fool if he doesn't recognise the spot he's in where you're concerned,' Madame le Brun insisted, and Willow frowned at her curiously.

'In what way?'

The shrewd eyes watched her for a moment, then the old lady nodded, as if convinced she was right about something. 'You find Adam attractive, don't you?'

Startled, Willow felt herself colour furiously, for she didn't like the trend of this conversation at all, although Madame le Brun seemed actually to be enjoying it. 'Adam's a very attractive man,' she allowed after a moment or two, and keeping careful control on her voice. 'I imagine most women find him attractive.'

'He's kissed you?'

Again Willow stared at her, although it was a statement rather than a question. She couldn't know anything, Willow told herself, but she trod carefully for all that, although it wasn't easy to prevaricate with that eagle eye fixed on her. 'I imagine he doesn't have any difficulty finding women willing to be kissed either,' she said, and the old lady snorted impatiently.

'Oh, come on, girl,' she told her brusquely. 'Do you think I don't know the signs? The way he looks at you, at your mouth especially, that's *always* a sure sign, and it was no brotherly peck either, if I know Adam!'

There was a curious curl of sensation in Willow's stomach, and she would have given a lot for the nerve to simply walk out of the room, but the old lady was used to getting what she wanted, and she wasn't likely to give up. 'You're taking rather a lot for granted, Madame le Brun,' Willow told her, 'and I don't think you have the right.'

'Nonsense!' Madame le Brun retorted. 'Why be ashamed to admit it? You already said you find him attractive, what more natural than that you should let him kiss you? Didn't you say he'd have no difficulty finding women willing to be kissed, why should you be any different?'

'Because I happen to be engaged to his brother, *madame*!'

'But he's not in much hurry to marry you, is he?' Madame le Brun insisted.. 'And it's my guess you're not a cold-blooded creature.'

'Neither of us is in a hurry,' Willow told her insistently, 'and it has nothing whatever to do with Adam! If *he* wants to marry somebody there's always Mrs Sai-Hung!'

'That woman!' Madame le Brun's lip curled derisively. 'Adam has too much pride to marry a woman who chases him like she does—he's a le Brun.'

'So was Richard's father!' Willow reminded her, and the old lady narrowed her eyes.

'Ah, Richard's told you about that, has he?'

'The second Mrs le Brun was a perfectly ordinary working girl from the sound of it, like me,' said Willow, refusing to be overawed. 'And the fact that your son married her proves that the le Bruns are as susceptible as ordinary men—frankly I find it rather a relief!'

'You're too smart by half, my girl,' Madame le Brun told her, but with a remarkable lack of animosity. 'It's that red hair; I warned Adam.'

'*Adam!*'

Willow spat it out with such ferocity that the old lady eyed her thoughtfully for a moment. 'I'd guess there was something a little more than just a kiss,' she said softly, and startled Willow with a sudden malicious chuckle. 'And I guess Richard had better move a little fast if he wants to make home base!'

That chuckle seemed to change the whole situation suddenly, and Willow found herself much less in awe of her. She was thoroughly enjoying putting the cat among the pigeons, and despite the uneasy moments she had given her, Willow couldn't help smiling ruefully as she shook her head. She had never visualised herself arguing with this autocratic old lady as she had been for the past few minutes, and she found it harder still to believe she answered her as she did.

'You're a wicked old woman,' she told her, and Madame le Brun nodded, not in the least deterred. 'You shouldn't talk like that to a stranger about your family.'

'If you're going to be one of us, you're not a stranger,' Madame le Brun argued, 'and I like you, Willow Grahame, even though you're not French.'

The confession was somehow oddly touching and Willow appreciated how much of an about-turn it must have been for her to admit it. 'I never could understand why Richard found you so fearsome,' she told her. 'I suppose it's being so different from Adam, and not so much like you.'

The old lady held out a hand to her, calling her across, and Willow once more felt a return of that earlier wariness as she obeyed. 'You're always so staunch in his defence,' Madame le Brun told her, and Willow shook her head.

'Wouldn't you expect me to be?'

'Do you love him?'

Willow looked down at her hands, and perhaps she did hesitate just a fraction too long before she replied. 'Yes, of course,' she said.

There was nothing said for a second, and then a hand was placed over hers and the thin fingers squeezed gently, watching eyes seeming to assess her possible reaction. 'I've had a hunch lately that you'd like to pull out of this so-called engagement—am I right?'

Hearing it said Willow wondered if the old lady was the only one to have noticed, and she caught her lower lip in her teeth for a moment. 'I have—thought about going home,' she confessed cautiously. 'I'd still keep in touch, but—I don't know, sometimes I feel that now Richard is involved in the Company he wouldn't mind quite so much.'

'You think he's cooling off?'

'I don't know—I don't think so, not exactly. But I had thought I might go home for a while.'

'Only?'

The gentle prompt made her shrug uneasily, for she wasn't about to admit to anyone as shrewd as Madame le Brun that there were things at La Bonne Terre that she would find hard to leave. 'I—I don't know; I just haven't got around to it.'

A bony finger reached up and lightly touched her cheek, making her look up automatically. 'Will you do something for me?' Madame le Brun asked very quietly, and Willow immediately sensed something in the way she spoke.

Nevertheless she nodded briefly. 'If I can, of course, *madame*.'

'Oh, you can,' Madame le Brun assured her, 'but the question is whether that tender conscience of yours will let you see straight for once.'

'I don't understand.'

'I guess you don't,' Madame le Brun agreed, 'but I'd like to see Adam married and settled down. I always planned for him to have a French bride, like his father had first off, but I've taken a fancy to you, my girl, I've taken your measure and I'd like to see him married to you.'

Too stunned for the moment to do anything but stare at her, Willow felt herself shaking like a leaf. The most stunning thing was to realise, once the initial shock had passed, that the emotional side of her was already viewing the proposal with more seriousness than she would have believed possible, and her heart was beating with the clamour of a drumbeat.

'I—I don't think you realise what you're saying,' she murmured eventually.

'Of course I realise,' Madame le Brun insisted. 'I'm not senile, girl!'

'But——' Willow's head was spinning; not least with the dizzying thought of Adam as a husband, and she tried hastily to put it away from her. 'I'm going to marry Richard!'

'Are you?'

Her pulse was racing because for the first time she considered the possibility of Adam knowing about his grandmother's scheme. For she could not imagine the old lady making such a direct approach if she did not have some kind of approval or authority from Adam, and at the thought of that being so her whole body trembled.

'He hasn't even bought you a ring yet, has he?' Madame le Brun pressed on relentlessly. 'Adam would have bought you a ring; you'd be in no doubt how *he* felt.'

But she was in doubt, Willow thought wildly. She was never sure what Adam meant with his kisses and his soft endearments, and invariably followed by a plea for her to give up Richard. 'I'm not *marrying* Adam!' she cried in exasperation, and almost stamped her foot for having allowed herself to be cornered like this. 'Please don't say any more about it, Madame le Brun!'

The old lady's speculative eyes regarded her steadily for a moment, then she shrugged. 'Very well,' she conceded, 'but you're being very silly.'

'I'm trying to be fair and honest *and* sensible,' Willow told her. 'From what I know of Adam he'd be horrified at the very idea of marrying me, and even more so at the idea of you saying anything to me.'

'I doubt it,' Madame le Brun denied confidently. 'And I doubt if you'll tell him!'

'I wouldn't dare!'

It was hard to believe that any of this was happening, and she certainly hadn't expected anything like it when she began what she thought would be a normal and pleasant morning, chatting and arranging flowers for the house. Obviously Adam *didn't* know anything about it, and she felt a sudden chill at the prospect of him ever finding out. It was difficult enough seeing him every day without this extra source of discomfiture.

Hearing a car door close outside, she looked up quickly, hoping against hope that it might be Richard come home. She badly needed his kind of almost offhand loving at the moment, although she would never dare tell him what had just passed between her and his grandmother. Even his customary awe of the old lady would banish in the face of that kind of provocation.

Hastily pushing the last rose into the vase, she gave Madame le Brun a brief glance over her shoulder before hurrying across the room. But it wasn't Richard she collided with in the hall, it was Adam, and her heart lurched so violently that it almost choked her when his hands clasped around the tops of her arms to help lessen the force of the collision. Her own hands were pressed to his chest and the feel of warm flesh through a soft silk

shirt stirred all the two familiar emotions into being so
that she hastily curled her fingers into her palms.

For a moment he said nothing, but stood looking down
into her face with his grey eyes half concealed by their
lids and the fringe of dark lashes. Then he glanced over
her shoulder at the door she had just closed behind her,
and a frown drew at his dark brows. 'What's wrong,
Willow? You look as if you're running away.'

'No, I'm not!'

She answered quickly and in a small breathless voice, and
his hands tightened on her arms, his frown deepening.
'You're shaking like a leaf, for heaven's sake! What's wrong?'

'I just—hurried, that's all. I—I thought I heard
Richard come back.'

'And you came running?'

There was mockery as well as concern in his eyes now,
and she shook her head, determinedly breaking the hold
he had on her. 'I came to meet him, that's all; didn't he
come back with you?'

He didn't answer immediately, but went on regarding
her with that steady and infinitely disturbing gaze, then
he stepped back and the heavy lids were down over his
eyes. 'He's on his way,' he told her quietly. 'Excuse me.'

His sudden coolness startled her, although she had so
determinedly put him away, and it struck her as she
watched him walk away from her that by making that
disturbing proposal Madame le Brun had put her into an
impossible position. She could no longer behave naturally
with Adam and she couldn't say anything to Richard
about it, she couldn't in fact confide in anyone, and she
felt quite alarmingly small and vulnerable suddenly.

'Your grandmother has a pretty poor opinion of Marsha
Sai-Hung, hasn't she?'

Willow put the question to Richard while they lazed
on the beach that afternoon, and he eyed her curiously
before he replied. 'Didn't I say so?' he reminded her, and
Willow nodded.

The quiet little beach was very relaxing, and she was feeling incredibly lazy, for she could still appreciate the novelty of lying under a palm tree on hot white sand with nothing to do but laze. The more popular and densely populated beaches of Honolulu did not appeal to her, but this quiet little haven that she and Richard used seemed to represent everything a tropical beach should be.

Lying flat on her back and with her figure revealed by the smallest of bikinis, she listened to the lulling shush of the surf and wondered what had possessed her to mention Marsha Sai-Hung. The same question had obviously occurred to Richard, for he turned over on to his stomach and looked down at her curiously, one fingertip tracing the line of her shoulder.

'What's the idea of bringing Marsha into anything?' he asked, and Willow shrugged.

'Oh, I don't know, she just happened to crop up in conversation this morning.' She sat up suddenly and shook the sand out of her hair, narrowing her eyes against the glare of sunlight on the surface of the sea.

'Talking about Adam?' Richard guessed, and she nodded.

'Talking about everybody really. You, me, Adam, Marsha—I was left in no doubt that Madame le Brun doesn't want Marsha at any price.'

She was treading on dangerous ground, she knew, but she felt oddly reckless at the moment, and that light fingertip of Richard's, now tracing down her back, made her shiver deliciously. 'Marsha's been divorced,' he reminded her, 'and Grand'mère's kind of stuck on old-time morality.'

With her feet curled around under her, Willow chose not to look at him. 'I think I must be to some degree,' she told him. 'If people want to divorce that's their affair, but personally I wouldn't like to go to my wedding backed up by the thought that I could always get a quick divorce if it doesn't work out just the way I want it.'

Richard's blue eyes were laughing at her, and he

reached up and curved a hand about her neck, pulling her down to him so that he could kiss her. 'I always figured you for a little puritan,' he accused, 'and I guess you just proved it!'

'Oh, I know why *you* think so,' Willow told him, drawing back. 'But I wouldn't like to think that you were consoling yourself with the thought of a quick divorce either.' He looked away at that, and it was all too reminiscent of other occasions when marriage had been mentioned, so that Willow's heart skipped anxiously. 'Richard?'

He sat up and put an arm around her, drawing her close to the naked warmth of his torso, and turning her to face him he kissed her mouth long and lingeringly. 'I'm not thinking of anything much at the moment,' he murmured against her ear, 'except loving you, you cute little puritan.'

She didn't like him calling her that, but she knew that if she protested he would simply laugh at her. But she did hold him off for a moment, and there was a slight frown between her brows when she looked at him. 'When are you going to think about getting married?' she asked, and the effect of the direct question was the same again, so that again she felt that curious little curl in her stomach.

Then he laughed suddenly and pulled her into his arms. 'I'm thinking about it,' he told her, and kissed her with such force she was gasping for breath when she eventually managed to wriggle free.

'Richard, I'm trying to talk seriously with you!'

She sat up, shaking her hair to remove the rest of the sand, and she sensed his curiosity, his dislike of the subject. He regarded her steadily and with a hint of hardness in his eyes she had never seen before. And even when he smiled again it wasn't with the same easy warmth as before.

'You're in a funny mood,' he complained. 'What's wrong, sweetheart, has Grand'mère been getting at you?'

'She—she asked me when we were getting married.'

'Oh hell, not again!' Willow watched him through her lashes and saw the slight thrust of his lower lip. 'Forget it, sweetheart—Grand'mère has a one-track mind, but she'll get tired one day.'

'I told her it was in the autumn,' Willow told him quietly, and met his frowning stare as steadily as she was able to.

'You did what?'

There was an edge on his voice that she chose to ignore. 'I thought it was time I made it something a bit more definite than my usual "don't know",' she told him, and when he didn't say anything, she put her head on one side and looked into his face. 'You don't sound very pleased.'

'I just don't like other folks poking into my affairs, that's all,' he said shortly, and Willow shook her head.

'Not even me?'

He didn't reply at first but looked at her with narrowed eyes, then he hugged her close again suddenly, and his voice was slightly muffled by her hair. 'You know how much I love you, sweetheart, I'd prove just how much if you'd let me. But please—don't try pinning me down with dates and plans, eh? Not when I have so much bugging me with the Company and all. And especially don't let Grand'mère hustle you into anything.'

'I wasn't exactly trying to pin you down,' Willow denied, but the quiet flatness of her voice must have told him how she was feeling. 'I just thought——'

'Sure, sure, I know!' He kissed her mouth lightly, then looked down at her and smiled with his usual confidence. 'Look sweetheart, you don't have to think about anything, leave it all to me, hah? You just go on looking beautiful and be around when I need you. O.K.?'

'*Do* you need me?' Willow asked, and he kissed her again.

'Sweetheart, of course I do!'

'But not enough to marry me?'

'Oh, Willow, sweetheart!' He studied her for a moment and she had never seen such speculation in his eyes before. Then he laughed, but it wasn't the usual lighthearted sound. 'Oh, baby, you're really putting the screws on, aren't you?' He kissed her, hard and forcefully, obviously intending to impress her with his confidence. 'You're not thinking of leaving me, are you?'

He was so sure she wouldn't, and in her heart Willow wondered if he wasn't right, at least in part. She had already admitted that she didn't want to leave La Bonne Terre, but she wished she was more sure of her reasons for wanting to stay. 'I had thought of going home, as a matter of fact,' she told him, and found herself waiting anxiously for him to decry the idea. Which was exactly what he did do.

'Not on your life!' he declared. 'You're not going home, I want you right here!'

'But if you're so busy, and you don't——'

'I want you right here,' Richard repeated firmly, and once more he pulled her into his arms, holding her there for several moments. Then a sudden deep sigh ruffled the top of her hair. 'O.K.,' he said, 'make plans for a fall wedding if that's what you want to do.'

It sounded much too much like a concession, and Willow raised her head again to look at him. 'You're sure it's what you want, Richard?'

He nodded, then laughed aloud and buried his face in her hair. 'If it makes you happy, go ahead,' he said, which Willow realised wasn't quite the same thing.

Richard had yet again gone to the Company office with Adam and, because she wanted to avoid being alone with Madame le Brun after yesterday's episode, Willow had gone into the garden. It was a pity that things had to change in that direction, for she had enjoyed being closer to the old lady, and she felt much too uncomfortable in her company now.

The garden never failed to delight her and she spent some time of every day out there, no matter how much Richard teased her about it. The enormous variety of scents and colours seemed slightly unreal to someone accustomed to the gentle flora of English gardens, and she knew it would be one of the things she missed most when she eventually went home.

Time always seemed to pass so quickly, even when she was obliged to amuse herself, and a pile of magazines had kept her occupied until she took her inevitable turn round the garden. She had one particularly favourite path; overgrown with the shrubs that bordered it and almost crowded out of existence by huge oleanders and the close-growing pink shower trees that scattered their blossoms at her feet like pink snow. As always when she was among these exotic bushes she was relaxed, and she was unaware of anyone else nearby until she turned at the end of the path to go back and found herself face to face with Adam.

Lips parted, she stared at him blankly for a moment, half deafened by the thudding beat of her heart. 'Did I startle you?' he asked.

That deep voice shivered over her skin like a caress, and Willow shook her head. A light blue shirt was stunningly effective with his tan, and he had abandoned the formality of a tie as he always did the moment he came home. Below the short sleeves, bare brown arms aroused memories that were best forgotten, and the dappling sunlight danced over a slightly bowed head.

He had discarded his jacket too, and fawn trousers fitted snugly over lean hips and long muscular legs, making him appear even taller than he was. Here under the trees his eyes looked darker than merely grey, and the lines of his face were deepened and more defined. His gaze, Willow noticed uneasily, was fixed on her mouth, just as Madame le Brun had remarked on. Even in this so far cool and polite mood he was a dangerously sensual and exciting man, and Willow despaired of her inevitable response to him.

'I—I didn't realise you were home yet,' she said, pulling herself quickly back to earth. 'Is Richard with you?'

She had asked him the same question yesterday, she recalled hazily, and he had treated it as a snub. Now he regarded her steadily for a moment and he must surely have noticed the faint flush in her cheeks. 'Is this another brush off?' he asked quietly, and the flush deepened.

'I don't understand you.'

'Oh, I think you do, Willow,' he argued. 'But if you're really anxious to know if Richard is home, he went straight into the house. I felt like a breath of air before lunch, so I came out here—I'm not really an indoor man, and I get a little stifled sometimes.'

It was an unexpected confession, and Willow wondered if he was feeling in a confiding mood, for he stood there with his hands in his pockets and looking very much at ease. 'Oh—yes, I see.'

The familiar glint of mockery showed in his eyes and Willow hastily looked away, for he could affect her all too easily even so. 'Which means you're not interested in my idiosyncrasies, and you'll slip away as soon as you decently can,' he guessed, then shook his head slowly. 'Poor Willow,' he went on, 'you keep finding yourself in—situations—with me, don't you? And you really don't like me very much!'

'That's not true!'

She denied it swiftly and without hesitation, and one of Adam's dark brows arched upwards. 'It isn't?' he asked, as if he was genuinely surprised. Then he shook his head again and held out a hand to her. 'Come on,' he said. 'Let's go see if lunch is ready yet.'

She didn't hesitate to take the proffered hand, but there was nothing she could do about the sudden violent lurch her heart gave when his strong fingers closed over hers. He didn't hurry, but set a strolling pace, pushing aside the overgrown shrubs and branches of fluffy pink blossom when it barred their way, and just for a moment Willow allowed herself to enjoy walking alongside him in a setting that was little short of idyllic.

They walked very nearly half-way back to the house in silence, and then Adam glanced down at her suddenly. 'I hear there's to be a wedding in the fall,' he said and, when Willow looked up at him swiftly, he raised his free hand in a gesture of conciliation. 'Don't get mad,' he begged in mock alarm. 'Grand'mère told me.'

Willow was praying that the old lady's revelations had stopped there, and she looked at him warily. 'I might have known,' she said.

If the old lady had even hinted at her alternative plan she didn't know how she was going to face him, and when he stopped suddenly and put a hand under her chin, her heart thudded anxiously and she hastily lowered her eyes. He said nothing for a moment, but looked down at her steadily. 'What made you tell her that, Willow?' he asked softly, and she glanced up just briefly through her lashes.

There were small tight lines at the corners of his mouth, she noticed, and a deep unfathomable look in his eyes that was infinitely disturbing. 'Because it's true,' she claimed, and again a dark brow arched in query.

'Is it?' His hand cupped her chin, and the soft ball of his thumb moved back and forth over her lips; a slow and sensual movement that once more stirred all those wild emotions into being. 'The way I figure it, Grand'mère was maybe pushing a little for the wedding date, and you said the first thing that came into your head. Then you broke the news to Richard when you visited the beach yesterday afternoon. Am I right?'

'Suppose you are?' Willow demanded.

She tried in vain to dislodge the fingers that curved about her jaw, but Adam quickly turned his hand and took hers instead, holding her firmly by both hands while he looked down at her. 'I thought so,' he said softly. 'Ever since last night, when you came back from the beach, he's looked kind of—shifty.' His thumb moved lightly across her mouth and there was something in his eyes that she dared not meet for too long. 'Willow, if he's trying to squirm out of it——'

'Oh no, no, he isn't—I'm sure he isn't,' Willow hastened to assure him, as anxious to convince herself as Adam, for she couldn't bear the thought of Richard really being as reluctant as he gave the impression of being. Nor could she face the idea of Adam believing his brother was being forced into something he didn't want.

He studied her for a moment, his eyes lighting on every feature in turn, but coming to rest inevitably on the soft and not quite steady fullness of her mouth. Then he nodded slowly, as if he wasn't entirely convinced. 'Just so long as he isn't trying anything on, and making you unhappy.'

She was so quiveringly aware of him as he stood there, virtually towering over her, that she wondered how much he really cared what Richard did. In fact he had done much more to make her unhappy than Richard had, but he wouldn't realise that. He was without doubt a much more practised lover than Richard was, and all too often she had allowed herself to come dangerously close to being seduced by his more mature sexuality.

It was the recollection of those moments that drove her so recklessly on, and she looked up at him through the thick shadow of her lashes in a way that was perhaps more provocative than she realised, her voice, light and breathless, challenging his claim to care. 'What would you do about it if you discovered Richard *was*—trying it on, and making me unhappy, Adam?'

He neither said nor did anything for several seconds, except tighten his hold on her hands, then he smiled suddenly, and the look in his eyes sent little tingling sensations right down to the soles of her feet. 'What would I do?' he asked softly, and his grey eyes, dark as storm clouds, rested on her mouth once more. 'Why, marry you myself, of course.'

Willow caught her breath and the colour flooded into her face. If she could have turned and left him she would have, but he still held both her hands, and he must feel how she was trembling. 'Adam——'

She tried to break his hold and move away, but he tightened his grip, holding her hands against the broad warmth of his chest where the steady beat of his heart echoed her own hard pulse. 'If you tease,' he murmured in a voice that fluttered like silk against her skin, 'you'd

better be ready to take what's coming to you.' When
she struggled he pulled her into his arms and held her
tight, but her struggles were only halfhearted and there
was no way he wasn't going to realise it. 'I guess you still
want to have your cake and eat it too, don't you?' he
said, and pulled her closer so that the warm, lean hardness
of him pulsed against her own trembling softness.

That now familiar look of desire burned into her as he
bent his head, and the stunning virility of him touched off
the same wild emotions she could never control, so that
when he touched his mouth to hers, her lips were eager
and parted, warm and responsive and offering no resistance at all. Her body bowed and yielded to the force of
his, and she lifted her arms to put them around his neck
and bring that savagely passionate mouth still nearer.

She scarcely believed it when only a second later he
put his hands on either side of her face and forced their
mouths apart, leaving her shaken and confused, and looking at him with clouded green eyes, as bewildered as a
child's, completely unaware as yet of any reason to bring
it to an end. Then Adam put her from him, though the
desire was still there in his eyes even when he glanced
aside, as if listening for something.

It was a moment or two before Willow registered the
light crunch of footsteps and thought of Richard, and she
stepped back. Her heart was rapping urgently, and there
was a bright warm colour still in her cheeks, and she had
time only to smooth down her dress and run a hand over
her hair before Richard appeared, walking around the
bend in the path and brushing aside the heavy boughs of
pink blossom before he spoke.

'Hey, what is this?' he greeted them cheerfully. 'Have
you forgotten lunch?'

He spoke without a trace of suspicion and Willow
wondered dazedly if it was conceit that prevented him
from even suspecting she would see Adam as anything
but his much older brother. At first the cheerful matter-
of-factness of his approach struck her as slightly unreal,

and it took her a moment or two to adjust to an entirely different situation.

Adam's recovery, on the other hand, seemed to be complete and almost immediate, and Willow was forced to recognise that this might not be the first time he had found himself in this particular situation. He smiled at Richard with no sign of unease beyond a trace of tightness in the lines at the corner of his mouth then, after a glance at his wrist-watch, he pursed his lips.

'I'll leave you two to make your own way back,' he said, 'but best not be too long if Grand'mère is waiting lunch. Oh, by the way, Richard,' he added with an air of apparent casualness that Willow found hard to believe, 'I hear there's to be a wedding in the fall.'

Richard's smile faded a little at that, and he glanced from Willow to Adam. 'Oh, you've heard, have you?' he said, and his lack of enthusiasm was such that not even the most insensitive person could have missed it.

'Not from you,' Adam remarked dryly. 'Grand'mère told me.'

'I didn't see the need,' Richard informed him. 'It's nobody's concern but mine and Willow's.'

'And Grand'mère's,' Adam reminded him with a faint smile. 'Though I wish it could have been a different time of year; we do have rather a lot on. Exactly when in fall were you thinking of?'

Before Willow could say anything, Richard gave a careless shrug. 'Makes no difference to me when it is,' he said.

'Or even if it isn't?' Adam suggested softly, and Willow caught her breath.

Richard looked so sheepish, in fact, that she wished the ground would open up and swallow her. They were discussing her marriage to Richard as if it was just another item to be fitted into the company's schedule, and after that kiss just a few moments ago, Willow felt tempted to disappear from La Bonne Terre for a while and sort out her own feelings, regardless of anyone else's. With Richard

being so offhand, Adam could almost be forgiven for suspecting that his brother's hand was being forced, and his
questioning the time she had chosen wasn't helping any
either.

'I hope you're not thinking of backing out,' Adam went
on in that devastatingly quiet voice of his. 'I have a per-
sonal stake in this particular wedding, as it happens.'
Richard looked immediately at Willow, but it was Adam's
glance that she noticed, for the expression in his eyes
stirred all those wild and alarming longings into being
again so that she hastily lowered her eyes. 'I made a promise that if you don't marry Willow as promised, I will;
so watch yourself, brother. O.K.?'

'You did *what*?'

Richard's glare did not deter him in the least and there
was a burning darkness in his eyes when he looked at
him, while Willow's heart thudded away almost in panic
as she stood helplessly by and listened to them. 'You heard
what I said,' Adam said coolly, and turned to go.

He went striding away from them along the path, and
when he disappeared from sight around the bend,
Richard was still staring after him. For her part, Willow
felt like running and hiding somewhere, for the situation
for her was rapidly becoming more than she could cope
with, and when Richard eventually recovered sufficiently
to turn back to her, she clenched her hands tightly to
help control her rising temper.

His eyes were narrowed and curious, and they showed
that same hint of hardness she had noticed on the beach
yesterday. 'What in hell was that all about?' he
demanded, and Willow shook her head.

It was unfair of Adam to have left her to explain, but
she had already reached the conclusion that her feelings
counted for very little. Absently touching a finger to her
lips, she shrugged and somehow managed to sound
matter-of-fact. 'Whoever knows what Adam is all about?'
she asked, and wished she knew herself.

CHAPTER EIGHT

WILLOW couldn't disguise her uneasiness, nor did she attempt to, when Richard spoke of staying on at La Bonne Terre; apparently he meant to go on as usual, no matter what happened. In normal circumstances she probably wouldn't have minded too much, but circumstances were hardly normal, and their staying on there could give rise to all sorts of difficulties. For one thing, she had the feeling that lately she had become rather less important in Richard's scheme of things, although he still laid claim to her with the same confidence. Then there was the prospect of living in such close proximity to Adam for years to come, and that was a situation she simply couldn't face, whatever else she had to contend with.

'I don't see what the hassle is about,' Richard observed. 'You like it here, don't you? You like the house and everything?'

'Yes, of course I do.'

She hesitated, not knowing quite how to go on, and Richard clucked his tongue impatiently. 'And you know how I feel about the old place. There's plenty of room for everybody and it's comfortable, so where's the problem?'

Willow used both hands in a vaguely helpless gesture and sought for reasons. 'I—just thought we might have had our own place after we're married, that's all. We've been through all this before, Richard.'

'I know it,' Richard retorted, 'and it makes no more sense now than it did then! Why the big issue, for God's sake?'

Willow didn't see how she could tell him that she couldn't go on living in the same house with Adam, and the more she thought about it the more certain she

became. Adam had taken up too much of her thoughts
lately. She had too often found herself putting him in
Richard's place, just as his grandmother had suggested,
and in view of Adam's expressed opinion of her that was
too ridiculous for words.

'Willow!' Richard heaved a great sigh, and it was obvious that he saw himself as sorely tried. Taking her hands
in his, he looked down at her with a hint of restrained
impatience. 'Look, sweetheart, I don't know what's running around in that cute little head of yours, but whatever
it is, forget it. I love you; you're sexy and you're beautiful
and I'd do just about anything to please you, you know
that. If you see yourself swanning down the aisle in miles
of white lace then go ahead and dream about it, baby.
But this one thing I do *my* way. No way am I moving out
of La Bonne Terre—O.K.?'

Because she knew he meant it, Willow nodded helplessly. She dared not tell him her reason, and without a
reason he wouldn't even consider moving away. He had
just told her so—adamantly. 'All right, Richard.'

But even Richard, it seemed, was affected by the quiet,
defeated air about her, and he pulled her into his arms
and kissed her—a kiss that she recognised was as firm and
unrelenting as his vow. 'Oh, come on, sweetheart, don't
look like I just broke your heart! You like it here, so
what possible reason could you have for not wanting to
stay, eh?'

Willow shrugged. 'None, I suppose.'

'Of course you haven't!' She couldn't look at him, and
even when he raised her face with a finger under her
chin, she kept her eyes downcast. 'It doesn't have anything
to do with Grand'mère, does it?' he asked, still trying to
find a cause for her reluctance, and Willow shook her
head.

'Oh no, I like her, we get along fine together.'

'Then what other possible——' He stopped there, and
Willow's heart thudded anxiously, for she could imagine
the way his eyes narrowed suddenly. Then he tipped her

chin more sharply, and when she looked up his eyes were gleaming wickedly with laughter. 'Well, what d'you know?' he drawled. 'I guess old Adam got to you after all, eh?' He laughed suddenly and kissed the tip of her nose. 'Oh, baby, I never thought you would!'

'Would what?' Willow breathed huskily, and for no good reason she felt a faint flutter of panic in her stomach. 'I don't know what you're talking about, Richard.'

'Adam,' he said, and laughed again.

Willow's colour was high, but she hoped he would put it down to annoyance rather than embarrassment, for he obviously wasn't treating it very seriously, whatever he said. Turning her head sharply, she avoided his hand. 'For heaven's sake don't be so idiotic, Richard! I don't find this particular joke very funny!'

'You don't?' He was still laughing, but it was hard to tell whether her annoyance affected him or not. 'But you'd be in good company if you did fancy him, sweetheart, he's quite a hit with the women. Although admittedly most of them are a little older than you and me,' he added with undisguised malice. 'Oh, come on, baby, admit you think he's got something!'

'I admit nothing,' Willow told him shortly. 'You're being childish and spiteful.'

'Oh, I am?' He eyed her for a moment. 'That's kind of strong, when I was only making a joke, isn't it, sweetheart? After all, if you did fancy old Adam it wouldn't be likely to last very long; you'd soon grow out of it, but you wouldn't be the first to have your toes curled by that sexy voice.'

'I don't—curl my toes over anything, and you're being rather matter-of-fact about it in the circumstances.' He raised a curious brow, and she went on. 'I *am* supposed to be your fiancée,' she reminded him.

'Touchy!'

He laughed and lightly kissed her mouth, and Willow somehow found the nerve to look at him directly. 'When you've quite finished making wild guesses,' she told him, 'I suggest we go back and get ready for dinner.'

Richard looked at her steadily for a moment or two as if he wasn't quite sure what to make of her mood, then he shook his head and pulled her into his arms. 'Oh, you are a sobersides,' he told her, pulling a glum face. 'Don't worry, sweetheart, I know you wouldn't give old Adam a second thought. Why should you? You've got me.' He meant it quite seriously too, Willow realised as he bent and kissed her mouth again. His hands pressed into the small of her back and when he looked into her eyes the words he said took on quite a different meaning. 'Oh, sweetheart, you don't know just how hungry I am,' he whispered.

Things seemed to have been happening with such bewildering suddenness lately, and Willow was finding this latest turn of events hardest of all to grasp. 'I couldn't believe it,' Richard was saying, and he laughed. A short nervous kind of laugh that suggested he really couldn't believe it.

He had been bubbling with excitement ever since he came back from escorting his grandmother on a walk around the garden, although he had been most reluctant to go, while Willow waited for him to take her into Honolulu. She had realised there was something the moment she saw his face when he reappeared, flushed and a little bewildered, his blue eyes shining with excitement. But she couldn't imagine what the old lady could have said to him that would have such an effect.

'We'll take a drive a little later, O.K.?' he asked, as he practically hauled her out into the garden, and Willow nodded.

'Yes, of course. Richard, what on earth is going on?'

'New York!' Richard crowed triumphantly, and looked impatient when she frowned at him blankly. 'I'm going to New York, Willow, to a job in a band, playing second guitar. It's all arranged!'

Just for a moment Willow had the curious feeling that she was going to be sick. Somehow she managed to keep a fairly firm hold on her facial expression, but her stomach was churning sickeningly. 'You—you've got a place in a band? In—New York?'

'Isn't it great? Grand'mère knows this guy who runs a club; kind of pseudo-Hawaiian but classy, he used to live here on the island and seemingly my pop knew him one time. I don't know how she did it, but Grand'mère got the word that he needed a player. His second guitar is quitting and he'll be needing a replacement; all I have to do is go—isn't it great?' Willow was too dazed still to see beyond the fact that Madame le Brun was working things out in her own way, and as far as she could see Willow's feelings were not to be taken into account. 'I'm to have a tryout for a couple of weeks,' Richard went on, 'and after that—nothing can stop me!'

From somewhere at the back of her spinning brain Willow picked on something practical, although she wasn't thinking very clearly yet. 'So you won't be with the company for very much longer?'

'Not on your life!' Richard laughed, and shook his head. 'Oh, Adam won't lose any sleep over it—I'm not exactly God's gift to big business, you know, and he'll probably heave a sigh of relief when I go.'

'I thought you were getting on rather well,' she suggested in a small voice, and yet again Richard laughed.

It was hard to realise that she could appear so outwardly cool when in fact her world had just been turned upside-down, but Richard was unaware of anything at the moment but his own triumph, and he had not so far made any mention of her place in the scheme of things. 'I'm good at putting on the act,' he told her, 'but even Adam's tolerance is wearing kind of thin lately. He wanted me in the company and I did what he wanted, now he knows how wrong he was. Another four weeks and he'll be begging me to take off for New York!'

'Very likely.' In fact at the moment Willow wasn't thinking so much of the effect on Adam or on the Company, but on her own life. She had come out to

Hawaii as Richard's fiancée, but it had become increasingly clear as the weeks passed that the relationship was a lot less stable than she had thought. Both Richard's and her own feelings seemed to have changed gradually, and her own in particular had given her a lot of cause for doubt lately. This latest bombshell, organised by Madame le Brun, seemed to be the last straw. 'I thought——' She passed a swift tongue over her dry lips and tried to bring herself back to practicalities. 'The other day you were so adamant about staying on at La Bonne Terre——'

'Sweetheart!' He hugged her close and he was smiling and so incredibly pleased with himself. 'I had no idea anything like this was in the offing then. This is too good to throw away, you must see that.' He was looking at her carefully controlled expression and frowning slightly. 'Oh, come on, Willow, don't look so discouraging. Another month and it will all start to happen!'

'I shall miss you.'

Willow made the statement with the deliberate intention of bringing him down out of the clouds for a few minutes, and when she saw his expression it was clear that until that moment he really hadn't given her a thought. He frowned uneasily for a moment, then pulled her into his arms again and kissed her.

'What's with missing me?' he demanded.

'Well, I'll be going home, naturally. I can't very well go on staying here.'

'Of course you won't, you'll come with me. We'll find an apartment some place; Grand'mère's pal can fix it.'

'No, Richard!'

'Why not?' Richard demanded, and the familiar thrust of his lip warned her that he wasn't going to like the argument she offered. 'What's to prevent you coming along too?'

'Four weeks isn't very long,' she said, and very carefully avoided mentioning marriage, although her meaning could have been in little doubt. 'I can't just go flying off to New York with you, Richard, you know that.'

'I know you *could*,' Richard insisted, his eyes stormily dark. 'But it's that same old rubbish, isn't it, darling? For crying out loud, Willow, will you get it into your head that nobody *cares* about that any more!'

'I care,' Willow argued in a small tight voice, 'and so does Madame le Brun, and I happen to value her respect.'

'More than you do my love, obviously!' Richard retorted harshly. Then, just as he always did, after a few moments he gave a great sigh of resignation and reached for her hands. 'Oh, look, sweetheart, don't spoil my big moment. This is just the chance I've been waiting for.'

Willow nodded, feeling rather small and lost suddenly, and a long way from home. 'Yes, I know it is, and I wouldn't want you to miss it. You have to go, I know that, Richard.'

'But without you along?'

He knew the answer to that, but he had made no suggestion that they should marry before he went, and it puzzled her for a moment that she felt a curious sense of relief because he hadn't. Nothing made much sense at the moment. 'That's up to you,' she told him quietly, and he looked at her as if he was only now beginning to grasp the fact that she really meant what she said about not going on his terms.

'I could—— –' he began, but stopped and looked around hastily when a shadow fell across the path beside them.

Willow too looked up, and there was something in Adam's grey eyes that she found oddly disturbing when he looked directly at her; almost as if he knew what they were arguing about. And she eased herself from Richard's arms almost guiltily. 'Sorry if I disturbed you,' Adam said blandly. 'I didn't realise you were here.'

Richard only glanced at him, then looked back at Willow, and his eyes were sharp and slightly narrowed as if he recalled that earlier conversation. 'Forget it,' he told Adam shortly. 'We've reached stalemate anyway!' He turned quickly and went stalking off back to the house without even attempting to persuade her to go with him.

'Trouble?' Adam asked quietly.

Willow turned back to him and shrugged uneasily, and there was something touchingly vulnerable about the slight droop of her shoulders. 'I suppose you've heard all about the job in New York?' she suggested, and Adam nodded.

'From Grand'mère. Is that what the trouble is?'

'Not exactly trouble,' Willow denied. She found it strange somehow that she felt able to confide in Adam of all people, but there was a kind of confident ease about him that suggested he would seldom back away from any situation, and she needed his kind of strength at the moment. Walking with him along the tree-shaded path, she tried to put her feelings into words. 'It's a wonderful opportunity for him, I realise that, but—well, it rather changes things. Between Richard and me, I mean. It's only four weeks until he's due to leave and it doesn't give us much time. Richard doesn't see the need—he doesn't——'

'See why you have to be married to go off with him,' Adam guessed dryly. 'I can imagine!'

She glanced at him, with a dark, vulnerable look about her eyes. 'You probably think I'm as old-fashioned as Richard does,' she ventured, and almost sighed aloud when he shook his head.

'I think nothing of the kind,' he told her in that deep and infinitely affecting voice of his. He walked beside her, matching his pace to hers, and as they passed under a big jacaranda the shadow of its feathery branches made it hard to discrn his expression, but his voice was gentle. 'I did try to warn you,' he reminded her, 'but you got the wrong idea of my motives, didn't you, Willow? He's already hurt you to some extent, but it could get worse——'

'Only if I let it,' Willow argued. By now it was second nature to react defensively to any criticism of Richard, and she didn't even stop to think about it. 'He isn't the

first man to get cold feet about getting married, and I
don't suppose he'll be the last.'

'I guess not,' Adam agreed quietly. He didn't actually
hold her hand, but his long fingers brushed lightly against
hers as they walked, and brought a curious kind of comfort. 'Don't get mad when I say this,' he said after a
moment or two, 'but is it marriage itself that's important
to you, Willow, or marriage to Richard?'

Willow didn't get angry, although she didn't quite
know why she didn't, and she chose her words very carefully. 'If you want the truth, I don't exactly know *how* I
feel at the moment,' she confessed, and realised when she
said it that as far as Richard was concerned it was quite
true.

'Bridal nerves?' Adam suggested, offering a way out,
and she laughed a little uneasily.

'It could be. But it's bound to come out right in the
end, isn't it?'

'All the best fairytales say so,' said Adam, and it seemed
the most natural thing in the world when he slipped his
arm under hers and bent briefly to kiss her cheek.
'Grand'mère is going to have her work cut out getting
you two sorted out,' he told her, but Willow said nothing
to that.

She couldn't help wondering if her feelings for Adam
weren't in even more need of sorting out than her relationship with Richard. But maybe Madame le Brun had
that in hand too.

For the whole of the following week Willow felt as if she
was living in a kind of limbo, not knowing quite what to
do, or what the eventual outcome would be. Richard was
acting very little differently towards her now that he had
recovered his temper, almost as if he hoped she would
eventually come around to his way of thinking. For he
hadn't once made a mention of marriage.

If she had any sense at all, she had told herself more
than once, she would leave Hawaii right then and go

home to England, but so far she had done nothing about
that either. The sensible thing to do would be to put her
engagement to Richard down to experience and forget all
about him. Adam she would find much harder to forget,
but that was another problem altogether, and one she
preferred to pretend didn't exist.

She was thinking along those lines one evening at
dinner when she became aware that Madame le Brun
was watching her closely, and when she glanced across
and smiled faintly, the old lady nodded. 'You'll wear
white, of course,' she said, and for a moment Willow gazed
at her blankly.

It was instinctive but quite inexplicable when she
looked across the table at Adam before she replied, although there was nothing to be read into that coolly enigmatic expression. 'I don't know, Madame le Brun. There's
some—I mean there may not——' She found the enquiring gaze of those shrewd old eyes too much suddenly, and
faltered. She felt such an abject coward for not having the
courage to tell them that there was a pretty good chance
she wouldn't be marrying Richard after all, but she simply
couldn't do it. 'It—it's a matter of time,' she finished
lamely, and knew that Adam was watching her now.

'Time?' The old lady poured scorn on the excuse, and
she gave Richard a sharp, narrow-eyed look that had him
shifting uneasily on his chair. 'Time has nothing to do
with anything, girl. A wedding can be arranged in no
time at all with the proper organisation, and I'm an ex-
tremely good organiser, even though some of you may
think me in my dotage.'

'Not me, Grand'mère!'

Richard was being an affectionate grandson suddenly,
but the old lady was not that easily fooled, and she quelled
him with a look before going on. 'I'll get Marie to make
you a wedding gown. She'll do it quickly to oblige me,
and it will be white, of course.' Her sharp eyes darted
between Willow and Richard. 'It will be appropriate, I
guess?'

Willow flushed and she didn't give Richard time to say anything, but once again glanced across at Adam. 'Yes, of course, *madame!*'

'Yes, of course,' Madame le Brun echoed with obvious satisfaction.

Richard was pulling a wry face, and he looked at his grandmother with a hint of challenge in his eyes, though he was not about to cross her too seriously with so much at stake. 'Do we have to have such depressing topics with dinner?' he asked facetiously, and laughed.

Madame le Brun looked at him for a moment with her head tipped back, and down the length of her aristocratic nose, although she was obviously less angry than might have been expected. 'There's nothing depressing about discussing your wedding, boy,' she told him. 'You're a lucky man to be getting a girl like Willow, and you should be happy she's marrying you.'

'I'd be happy if she'd just settle for loving me,' Richard told her, taking a chance, and Willow sensed rather than saw Adam's head come up sharply.

'Isn't it possible to do both?' he asked quietly, and his eyes were on Willow when he said it. Shadowed and half hidden, but curiously gentle. 'And give a little thought to how Willow feels hearing you talk as if getting married to her is the worst kind of punishment, will you?'

Richard's eyes narrowed, looking across at him for a moment with a dark, malicious gleam in his eyes. 'Are you taking brotherly care of her?' he asked in a voice that was a harsher imitation of Adam's soft tones.

Adam's control was superb, and while Willow almost held her breath on the outcome, he finished the mouthful of food he had before saying anything. 'I don't like to see a nice girl hurt,' he said with devastating quietness. 'And for some reason best known to her, Willow wants to get married to you, something you don't seem to appreciate.'

Richard hesitated. He never liked pitting his arguments against Adam, and he was in no mood to take any more chances with his grandmother's patience. Inevitably he

backed down, laughing shortly. 'O.K., O.K.! I submit to
the wedding bells if it will make Willow happy. You don't
have to look like you mean to take me apart, Adam, for
God's sake!' He turned to Willow and gave her one of his
most engaging smiles. 'Sorry, baby—forgive me?'

It would have been difficult to do anything else, and
Willow gave him a faint smile. She wanted nothing so
much as to have the subject dropped as soon as possible,
and she hoped this would be an end of it. 'You're forgiven,' she told him.

But it was a vain hope to think that Madame le Brun
was going to abandon her favourite topic so soon, and she
was already planning her next move. 'I shall see Marie
tomorrow,' she stated firmly. 'It won't be necessary for
you to come with me, Willow; just give me your measure-
ments and leave everything to me. I'm sure your mother
will forgive me if I take this on myself instead of leaving it
to her as is normal. I'd like to make the gown a wedding
gift, and I'm sure she'll understand.'

'That's very kind of you, Madame le Brun, and I'm
sure Mum won't mind, but——'

'I'll hear no arguments,' the indomitable old lady
declared. 'You'll write and let your folks know about the
change of date, tell them it's been brought forward to—
we'll check the exact date after we're through dinner, and
you can let them know in plenty of time. We can put
them all up here, so there's no problem about that, and
anyone else you want to ask, of course. I'll see the caterers
and the florist too.'

She was making mental notes as she went along, Willow
realised a little dazedly, and marvelled at the sharpness of
that aged brain. But it was all going so fast that Willow
found herself trying to quell a flutter of panic as she
listened to her. She saw her own future being planned for
her step by step, relentlessly, and she wasn't at all sure
that it was the future she wanted. Although at the moment
she hadn't the nerve to say so.

'Getting the gown is the first thing,' Madame le Brun

went on. 'It's possible Marie will have a ready-made to fit you, but if she hasn't then it will have to be made.'

She broke off and looked up with a faint frown when Willow spoke. 'Madame le Brun——'

'Oh, and you'd better start calling me Grand'mère, then you'll be used to it by the time you join the family. Try it, girl.'

Feeling very much as if she had been trapped, Willow took a breath and did as she was told. 'Grand'mère,' she said.

'Not bad,' the old lady told her, 'although you'll have to get Adam to correct your accent.'

Willow glanced up in time to see her give Adam a long, meaningful look, and at once the colour flooded into her cheeks. He couldn't possibly have the faintest idea that his grandmother would rather he was marrying her than Richard, but knowing what she did Willow was alarmed at how close to the wind the old lady was sailing.

Adam, for his part, was looking at his grandmother and shaking his head, and his grey eyes had that deep, cloudy look that Willow was all too familiar with. 'Take it easy, Grand'mère,' he told her quietly. 'You're kind of rushing things along, and——'

'I know what I'm about,' Madame le Brun interrupted firmly, then pressed her own bony hand over his with an affection there was no mistaking. 'Take my word for it, my dear, I know what I'm about.'

'I wish I did,' Richard grumbled darkly. 'Suddenly this wedding caper is taking off like there was no tomorrow!'

'There aren't enough tomorrows,' his grandmother informed him, but he shrugged and turned to Willow.

'Have a heart, darling, do we have to have all this stuff? The gown and the preacher and all that jazz?'

'But of course you'll be married by a preacher,' Madame le Brun told him indignantly, and before Willow could make her own reply. 'Right here at La Bonne Terre, like the le Brun weddings always are. What a Philistine you are, Richard!'

'It seems to me,' Richard complained bitterly, 'that I'm just getting hauled along with this circus whether or not I want to go! Don't I get *any* say in it?'

'You can say "I will",' Adam told him in his deep and dangerously quiet voice, and Richard held his gaze for only a moment.

'Thanks a lot!' he muttered sarcastically.

Willow was beginning to realise that he was being bull-dozed along in much the same way as she was herself, and she felt rather sorry for him suddenly. She doubted if he had any idea how uncertain she was of her own feelings and about the wedding, but the situation was becoming more and more complicated by the minute and she wished she could see a way out. It was instinctive when she reached out and touched his arm.

'Richard.'

He turned and looked down into her face, and in all probability he completely misread the sympathy he saw in her eyes. 'I always figured I could talk you out of the bells and rice,' he confessed ruefully, 'and I might have too, if the family hadn't muscled in on the act!' He sighed in sympathy with himself, then made the inevitable gesture of resignation. 'O.K., go ahead with your circus. I've got a couple of weeks to get used to the idea—or do the other thing!'

It could have been the way out she had been looking for, Willow realised, but too late; Adam forestalled her. He looked at Richard across the width of the table and his eyes glittered in a way that made Willow shiver suddenly. 'You just try anything as dirty as ditching Willow at the last minute,' he gritted, 'and I'll destroy you, Richard, I swear it!'

The threat in those thunderously grey eyes and the quiet menace of his voice startled Richard so much that he simply stared at him in stunned silence. He looked briefly at his grandmother, and not at all at Willow, then subsided, picking up his fork again to get on with his meal. Willow, hastily biting her lip, looked down at her hands clenched tightly and resting on the table, and only Madame le Brun was smiling. She sat at the head of the table nodding her head and her small brown face wrinkled with a smile that made her look incredibly sly and knowing.

It was only a day or two later, and very early in the morning, when a package arrived for Madame le Brun from Marie, her couturier in Honolulu. Willow was still eating her breakfast when she had a summons to join the old lady in her room, and it was a command that could not very well be ignored.

Despite everything she felt a thrill of excitement as she made her way upstairs, for it wasn't every day that a girl had a wedding dress bought for her from one of the most expensive salons in town, whether or not she would eventually wear it as a bride. She found the old lady out of bed and very elegant and French in a silken robe and a sleeping cap, and her eyes gleamed with anticipation as she signalled her right into the room.

The box was already open on the bed with its clouds of tissue paper laid back, and as Willow walked into the room Madame le Brun turned and lifted out the contents, holding it up in her gnarled hands for her to see. Willow felt a lump in her throat, for it was the most exquisite thing she had ever seen and the thought of *not* wearing it almost broke her heart.

'Put it on, girl,' Madame le Brun instructed, and Willow took it almost reverently.

A few moments later she stood in front of the old lady's dressing mirror and looked at herself, and no matter what its arrival implied Willow found it difficult to harden her heart against taking it. The pure whiteness of it added lustre to her creamy skin, and her shining copper-red hair was in stunning contrast, so that it was like seeing a stranger looking back at her—an exotic stranger who smiled a little dazedly at her own faintly flushed cheeks and bright green eyes.

Madame le Brun was as excited as a child and her eyes were bright and shining with a shimmering kind of warmth. 'You look beautiful, child,' she told her softly. 'Just beautiful. Marie can always be relied on to know what's right, and she's excelled herself this time; I shall tell her so.'

'It *is* beautiful.' Willow stroked her hands down the skirt, thrilling to the touch of pure silk and snowy lace.

'You're pleased with it?'

'How could anyone not be?' Impulsively she turned and put her arms around the old lady and kissed her cheek, coping with a sudden mistiness in her eyes. 'I've never seen anything so lovely before.'

'Let's hope Adam thinks so too,' said Madame le Brun, and Willow did not even try to pretend it had been a slip of the tongue.

'It's Richard I'm marrying, Madame le Brun,' she corrected her quietly, but her heart was racing like a wild thing as she again caught sight of her image in the mirror and imagined Adam instead of Richard standing beside her.

'So you keep saying,' Madame le Brun remarked with a touch of tartness, 'but it seems to me that young man isn't too keen on getting married,' She noticed Willow about to say something and held up a hand. 'However, whoever you marry, you'll make a very lovely bride, my girl, and one the le Bruns can be proud of.'

Willow looked at her fondly and shook her head. 'And I know that coming from you that's quite a compliment,' she told her softly. 'Thank you, *madame*.'

'I'm glad you realise it,' the old lady told her blandly. 'And haven't I asked you to call me Grand'mère?'

'I'll try and remember,' Willow promised, and turned once more to the mirror, drawn irresistibly by what she saw there.

Her reflection shimmered like a dream before her, and she caught her breath suddenly when another figure appeared in the long mirror as well as her own. A tall, shadowy figure in the background, that set her pulse racing hard as she stared at him with slightly dazed green eyes, and her lips parted.

The door was ajar and he stood just outside it on the landing, his face half in shadow but with that searing look of desire in his eyes that made her head spin as she watched him widen the opening and step just inside the room. Quite automatically she smoothed her hands down over the softness of silk, following the soft contours of her own body, and Adam's eyes followed every inch of the way.

For a few breathless seconds it seemed as if the two of them were suspended in time, and Willow felt a wild uncontrollable surge of elation while he held her gaze. For a breathtaking moment it was almost as if he had touched her physically with those long brown hands, and she passed the tip of her tongue slowly over her lips.

'Willow!'

His deep voice was so quiet that it barely reached her, and she was unaware that she was smiling in the way she did, a slightly appealing yet infinitely provocative smile that showed more in her eyes than on her lips. And his gaze moved inevitably to her mouth and lingered there.

It was a slight involuntary movement of Madame le Brun's that broke the spell, and with one hand to her breast to try and steady the violence of her heartbeat, Willow slowly shook her head. Very reluctantly Adam's eyes moved from her reflection and turned to his grandmother, but his voice still had that same deep, shivering timbre.

'Mrs McKendrick is on the line for you, Grand'mère, will you speak with her?'

'Of course I'll speak with her,' his grandmother told him. 'Why didn't you put the call through here instead of coming all the way upstairs?' Then she tilted her head to one side and gave him one of her small sly smiles, waving her hands dismissively. 'O.K., I know why—you wanted to get a look at Willow in her wedding dress. I guess

Luana told you it had arrived.'

'As a matter of fact I wasn't sure you were awake yet, and I didn't want to disturb you by letting the phone ring if you were still asleep.' He made the explanation logically enough, but he never once took his eyes off Willow while he made it, and quite clearly his grandmother didn't believe a word of it. Catching Willow's eye for a second, he smiled in a way that once more set her heart thudding like a drumbeat. 'But it was worth the trip upstairs to see Willow in her wedding dress.'

'And having seen her,' Madame le Brun told him with a gleam of satisfaction in her eyes, 'you can get right on out of here and put my call through. Go on, shoo! Don't you know it's bad luck for you to see the bride in her gown before the wedding day?'

Once more Adam's cloudy grey eyes caught Willow's gaze via the mirror and he shook his head slowly. 'You've got your lines crossed, Grand'mère,' he told her. 'I'm not Richard.'

'Just for once I wish you were!' Madame le Brun retorted, and Willow saw the way Adam's eyes narrowed suddenly when he looked at her. But the old lady had had her say and she was once more ushering him from the room. 'Get out of here and put my call through,' she told him, 'before Alice McKendrick thinks I'm still abed.'

Adam said nothing, but before he turned to go he again sought and held Willow's eyes, and it was as if she felt that firm sensual mouth on hers when his gaze rested there for a moment before he went out. He closed the door very quietly behind him, and it was a second or two before Willow was brought swiftly back to earth by Madame le Brun's light touch on her arm.

'Better get changed, my dear,' she suggested, and her shrewd eyes took note of the soft warmth of colour in Willow's cheeks and the glowing greenness of her eyes. 'I hope you're not superstitious,' she said, and Willow shook her head.

Standing there in such an exquisite dress it wasn't easy

to outface the indomitable old lady who had provided it for quite a different reason than either of her grandsons guessed, but Willow made an attempt nevertheless. 'As Adam said, Madame le Brun, you've got your lines crossed. That superstition applies only to the bridegroom, and if I ever wear this dress it will be when I'm married to Richard.'

The telephone by her bedside gave a faint ping, but although she spared it a brief glance, Madame le Brun looked back at Willow again. Her sharp old eyes gleamed knowingly as she walked over to the bed, and she was nodding her head. 'We'll see,' she said as she reached for the instrument. 'We'll see.'

CHAPTER NINE

IT was rather unsettling for Willow during the next few days, because she wasn't sure what to do for the best. Richard talked incessantly about his prospects in New York and seemed interested in little else, certainly not in wedding plans, so that Willow was becoming more and more convinced that the whole thing ought to be called off before it went any farther.

The thought of never being able to wear her beautiful wedding dress saddened her, but losing the chance to wear it was better than making a mistake of the magnitude it would be if she went ahead and married Richard. In fact it was really only Madame le Brun's persuasion that kept her still at La Bonne Terre; that and the thought of losing all contact with Adam.

It was at lunch one day that things finally came to a head. Madame le Brun was, as usual, making plans for the wedding, and Willow felt suddenly that she couldn't let the charade go on any longer. And it had become a charade, there could be no doubt about that, for she didn't want to marry Richard, and the more she thought about it the more certain she became.

'Now, Willow,' Madame le Brun said, 'have you written your parents and told them the change of date?'

Willow took a deep breath. 'No, *madame*, I haven't.' She looked at Richard appealingly, hoping against hope that she wasn't going to make too much of a hash of things now. 'If I could just say something.'

'Why, of course, girl,' the old lady encouraged her. 'What is it?'

Madame le Brun's shrewd eyes were watching her, and so, she realised, were Adam's, but now that she was faced with the immediate need to put it into words Willow felt a small flutter of panic, and she bit her lower lip anxiously. 'I—I realise how much trouble you've gone to, *madame*,' she began, 'and don't think I don't appreciate it. You've bought me that lovely wedding gown, but—well, you see——'

'What she's trying to say,' Richard interrupted with a short laugh, 'is that there isn't going to be any wedding; right, sweetheart? I never liked the idea and Willow has finally come around to my way of thinking. Ditch all the fuss and stick to the basics!'

'Damn you, Richard!'

Adam's anger was startling in its vehemence and Richard started visibly, his eyes fixed warily on his brother's dark, stormy face. Willow was looking at him more anxiously for she felt she knew Adam well enough now to know that it would be useless trying to explain that she felt a sense of relief because the folly of that makebelieve engagement was finally at an end.

He was never going to believe that she was thankful it had happened, because he was still convinced that Richard was jilting her, and he would see anything she said along those lines as simply a way of saving face. Also when Adam was as angry as he looked now he wasn't a man to try and reason with.

Richard put down his knife and fork with wary deliberation, and his good-looking features were set stub-bornly, because he was so sure he had her support at last. Willow dreaded the thought of him and Adam quarrelling when there wasn't any cause, but it wouldn't be easy to intervene at that point.

'Willow's known my feelings all along about this wed-ding nonsense,' Richard declared, and Adam's brooding grey eyes were turned in her direction.

'Is that true, Willow?'

His quiet voice was in such contrast to the look in his eyes that she found it impossible to do other than tell him the truth. 'Not quite all along,' she denied. 'But just lately—I began to realise about a couple of weeks ago that Richard—that he wasn't keen on the idea of getting married.'

'I'm keen enough on you,' Richard insisted, anxious that there should be no mistake about that. 'I just don't go for all that other junk, that's all. I just want you to come to New York with me without all the hassle of get-ting married first.'

'Are you saying that you never intended getting married?' his grandmother asked, in much the same quiet voice that Adam had used, but without the suppressed anger. 'You're telling me that you were never engaged to Willow?'

Richard's blue eyes were lowered for a moment, and he shrugged with seeming carelessness. 'I guess not.'

'But you, Willow?' The old lady shifted her gaze. 'You didn't take it that way, hmm? You really thought you were engaged to be married to Richard?'

Willow couldn't bear the thought of anyone feeling sorry for her, and she instinctively angled her chin when she looked at the old lady. 'Even the brightest of us can be naïve on occasion,' she said in a small husky voice, 'and I've never claimed to be a genius!'

Richard was looking at her as if, at least for the moment, he regretted having said what he did. 'I'm sorry, sweetheart,' he said, 'but I never figured you taking it that seriously until you started talking about—after we're married. That engagement talk before we came out here was——'

'So that Willow would be sure to come with you,' Adam guessed in a flat cold voice, and his obvious opinion brought a flush to Richard's face.

'Well, what of it?' he demanded, and seemed to take encouragement from the fact that his grandmother wasn't as angry as he had expected, although he could scarcely have known why. 'What's so bad about resorting to a little subterfuge?' he asked Adam defiantly. 'It worked, didn't it?'

'It worked!'

The harshness of Adam's expression made him look very much older suddenly, and Willow wondered if it wasn't time she intervened before their quarrel became more bitter and serious. She should let Adam know that he had no need to be so fierce in her defence because she was no more anxious to marry Richard than he was to marry her, though for quite different reasons.

By the time she had summoned sufficient courage to speak up, however, Adam was already taking up arms again, and however much she regretted his fighting with his brother it gave her a strange sense of satisfaction that he did so. 'You've done some pretty selfish things in your time,' he said in a voice that was edged with steel, 'but this is the dirtiest so far!'

It was obvious to anyone that he was holding a pretty formidable temper in check, and Richard must be aware of it, so that there was a kind of defensiveness even in his exasperation. 'Oh, for God's sake! This concerns me and Willow, and Willow isn't griping, so why should you?'

'Willow?'

The deep quiet voice slid along her spine, seeking her confirmation, and those clouded grey eyes were turned on her once more; enquiring and compassionate, so that she hastily looked away. His pity was unbearable suddenly, and she got to her feet, letting her knife and fork fall with a clatter on to her plate.

'It doesn't matter,' she said, in a husky voice. 'Please don't worry about it, Adam.' Obviously her response puzzled him, for to her relief he said nothing, only followed her with his eyes all the way to the door.

'Darling, where are you going?'

That was Richard, of course, not yet able to grasp that she had just made it quite clear how she felt. When he started to get up from the table she half-turned her head and looked at him steadily for a moment from the doorway. 'What does it matter?' she asked, and laughed shortly when she saw the way his expression changed. 'I don't want to marry you, as it happens, Richard, but I'm even less interested in your alternative proposal. I'm not sure I ever did want to marry you, when I think about it—and please don't follow me!'

'Willow!'

She had a good start and it gave her a great deal of satisfaction to slam the door when he was no more than half-way across the room. She had only a second before the door banged behind her, but during that time she noticed that Madame le Brun had a restraining hand on Adam's arm and was shaking her head slowly.

Willow didn't really care where she went when she left the dining-room, she just wanted to be alone for a while and try to sort out her tangled emotions. Getting away from La Bonne Terre was no longer something she could allow to loiter in the back of her mind, it was imperative that she leave as soon as she possibly could, and she needed to think out her next move in peace and quiet.

It was almost inevitable when she made for her favourite path through the shrubbery, but she had not gone very far before she realised she had been followed after all. 'Willow!'

She ignored Richard's call and rued the fact that she wasn't going to get the respite she needed. She simply went on walking, but sooner or later he was bound to catch up, and she could hear him coming after her, his breathing hard and uneven as if he had been running, which suggested Madame le Brun had detained him too, for as long as she could.

'Hang on, sweetheart, will you?'

Still Willow went on ignoring him, not even turning her head but walking on past the crowding oleanders and under the shower trees that scattered their pink blossoms in her hair. It was remembering that she had walked there with Adam that made her catch her lip between her teeth suddenly before she shook her head over things that were best forgotten.

'Hold it, will you! Quit playing hard to get, Willow!' Richard grabbed her arm and forced her to a standstill, but despite his tone his eyes suggested that he expected some kind of a welcome.

Instead Willow took a long hard look at him and realised that she was really seeing him for the first time, and not altogether liking what she saw. He was very good-looking and undeniably attractive, which was perhaps most of the trouble with Richard, for he knew exactly what his assets were and blatantly used them to his own advantage. It had never occurred to her before just how utterly selfish he was, yet it shouldn't really have come as such a surprise.

'I'd rather like to be alone, if you don't mind, Richard,' she told him quietly, and she was thankful to notice how calm and unruffled she sounded.

'Ah, come on, I only want to walk along with you!'

The look in his eyes showed that he expected her to agree, and he stared at her in astonishment when she suddenly laughed aloud. With the back of a hand to her mouth she looked at him for a moment, and she would have been the first to admit that it was malice that made her eyes gleam the way they did.

'You just never give up, do you, Richard?' she said, and he shook his head dazedly.

'I don't get you,' he said, then frowned when she

laughed again. 'And for God's sake stop laughing like that!'

'Don't you think it's funny?' she asked.

'No, I damned well *don't* think it's funny when you stand there laughing like an idiot when I'm trying to talk seriously with you!'

'Seriously?' Willow appeared to be giving the idea some thought, but she still had that curious sense of elation, although she couldn't account for it. 'Were you ever serious about me, Richard?'

'You know I was,' Richard protested. 'I still am, damn it.'

'But not enough to marry me?' Willow didn't wait for an answer, but shook her head at him and walked on again. But once again she did not get very far before he caught up and took her arm again in a grip that dug hard into her flesh. 'I remember,' she went on, 'that you told me, when we were driving out here from the airport on the day we arrived, that neither you nor Adam were the marrying kind. I should have realised then how true it was and seen through our so-called engagement as nothing but a—a con trick to get me to come with you.'

'O.K., O.K., I've admitted it, haven't I?' It was hard to judge the look in his eyes, but his customary confidence lurked not too far in the background. Richard could never see when he was beaten. 'Oh, come on, sweetheart, I used the engagement as bait and you fell for it, but hell—a guy in love is allowed a few little tricks, isn't he?'

'Is he?' Willow sounded far more casual than she was feeling. 'You may find it very naïve of me, Richard, but I honestly believed I was engaged to you, and to me being engaged means being able to——'

'Hear wedding bells!' Richard jeered, and she flinched inwardly at the thought of having been so completely fooled.

'I was going to say trust one another,' she corrected him quietly, and just for a moment he had the grace to look sheepish. 'Of course I did expect to marry eventually; it's the usual outcome of an engagement.'

'Well, I don't think that way,' Richard declared.
'When I say love, I mean somebody to share my life with,
not being bound hand and foot by a piece of paper!'

'Someone you can conveniently forget about when
someone more interesting comes along?' Willow suggested
quietly. 'I'm sorry, Richard, but you know my feelings
about your kind of loving.'

'I've heard it often enough,' Richard declared. 'But
you must know it wouldn't be like that for us, Willow. I'd
never walk out on you, I love you.'

'I'm quite sure you don't,' she argued mildly. 'Oh, I
know you've said it often enough, and you've tried often
enough to do what you like to term—prove it to me. But if
you loved me, Richard, you wouldn't have found the idea
of marrying me such an ordeal. I can only think that you
just couldn't face the prospect of being tied to me for the
rest of your life, and you left your grandmother and Adam
in no doubt of it either. Quite frankly, I'm grateful to you
for speaking out when you did.'

'Grateful? Richard stared at her uncertainly. 'What are
you getting at?'

'I'm grateful that you made me see you as you really
are. If you hadn't defied your family's attempts to make
you marry me I'd have found out too late that I don't
really like you very much, Richard.'

'Oh, you don't?' His hand tightened its hold on her
arm, and there was a hint of cruelty in the set of his
mouth that was completely out of character for the
Richard she had thought she knew. 'Well, get this, sweetheart, you were never in any danger of being married to
me because I'd never have stood for that bridegroom
nonsense whoever put the heat on! No way would you
have got me in front of a preacher, baby, I promise you!'

'Oh yes, I realise it now,' Willow admitted, in a voice
she did her best to keep steady. 'I only wish I'd realised it
before this.'

'So—we finally got that little schemozzle cleared up!'
He laughed shortly and without humour, and his eyes were

bright and glittering; resentful, she thought, as well as
angry, for Richard was proud of his reputation as a char-
mer. 'Wow, you really are a little puritan, aren't you? I
figured it was a front and I could talk you around to my
way.' He eyed her with glittering speculation for a
moment, then smiled. 'I guess I might have gotten away
with it too if I hadn't brought you here.'

'I think not,' Willow assured him. 'You wouldn't have
got away with it as long as you did if I'd listened to Adam.
He kept telling me I should give you up before I got hurt,
but I didn't trust his motive. I thought he saw me as a
fortune-hunter.'

'Adam?' His eyes narrowed, and dark with resentment,
sending a warning trickle along her spine; but realisation
came too late. 'So *that's* it!' His sudden bark of laughter
made her flinch as if he had struck her. 'I once said you
fancied him, and I guess I was right! You're not letting
go the le Brun millions, are you, sweetheart? You're just
changing partners!'

'Richard, you're talking nonsense!'

'Like hell! You've always given old Adam the eye, but
you're out of your tiny mind if you think he's any more
marriage-minded than I am, however much pressure he
puts on me! You figure that if I won't marry you, he will?
No way, baby! You're way out of your class with him!'

'Richard, stop it, please!'

It suddenly wasn't possible to remain calm any longer,
and to her dismay Willow felt the warning prickle of tears
in her eyes. Richard's brash judgment had made her realise just how right he was, for not until this moment had
she realised just how much Adam meant to her, and she
felt very small and lost suddenly.

She had to leave La Bonne Terre as soon as possible,
before Adam came to the same conclusion Richard had
and began to feel sorry for her. She couldn't bear to see
that look of pity and compassion in his eyes again as she
had when Richard so relentlessly turned down the idea of
marrying her. It wasn't pity she wanted from Adam, and

there was little chance of her getting anything else.

Perhaps her obvious vulnerability touched even Richard's selfish heart, for he reached out for her and would have taken her into his arms, murmuring something under his breath. But Willow turned from him swiftly and went running back towards the house, blindly and instinctively, for it wasn't Richard's arms that she wanted around her at that moment.

By dinner that evening Willow was feeling a little more composed, although every nerve in her body tingled at the thought of sitting across the table from Adam while she said what she had to say. For she went in to dinner with the firm intention of telling Madame le Brun that she would be leaving Hawaii by the first available plane; she hoped some time during the following day.

In the event it proved even more difficult than she feared to summon the necessary aplomb to break the news, and she was conscious more than once during dinner of Richard eyeing her speculatively, as if he was wondering what her next move was going to be. And several times too Madame le Brun tried to catch her eye; an invitation she avoided until she felt confident of being able to handle the announcement without making a complete fool of herself. Most of all she avoided looking in Adam's direction in case she weakened and backed off from taking the step that would take her away from him for good.

Her opportunity came as they were all preparing to leave the table at the end of the meal, and she stated her intention in a clear voice that wavered only a little. 'I shall be leaving some time tomorrow, Madame le Brun,' she said, and at once everyone was still, caught in the act of getting up from the table. She went on more quickly and breathlessly, avoiding the grey eyes that looked up swiftly and tried to catch her gaze. 'I've decided that the sooner I go home to England the better it will be for everyone, but I'd like you to know that I'm very grateful to you, *madame*, for making me so welcome and being so kind. I have—enjoyed it despite—everything, please believe that.'

'My dear child!'

Madame le Brun's sympathy was almost her undoing, but she pressed on even though it was becoming increasingly difficult to control her voice, and there were tears prickling at the back of her eyes so that she kept them downcast. 'I—I know you'll understand why it's so—so sudden, but——' She swallowed hard and shook her head in despair of being able to finish what she had to say before she started to cry. 'As—as I have quite a lot of packing to do—will you excuse me?'

'Willow!'

It was hard to believe that Richard sounded reproachful, but she wasn't really interested in him at the moment. From the corner of her eye she noticed Madame le Brun lay a hand on Adam's arm in that gently restraining gesture she had used on another occasion, and she heard Adam's almost inaudible sigh of resignation.

'Of course we understand,' he said in that quietly beautiful voice that had been the first thing she found attractive about him. He would have said more, Willow thought, but instead he shook his head almost impatiently and was silent.

The stairs offered an easy way of escape, and Willow hurried across the hall towards them, only to be halted after a few steps by Adam's voice. The fact that he had followed her suggested he had ignored his grandmother's advice after all, and Willow came to a halt at the foot of the stairs. He came up behind her and strong fingers closed tightly over hers where they rested on the balustrade, and even now she felt an upsurge of excitement at the touch of him.

'What have you done about booking a place on a plane?' he asked, and for a moment the sheer practicality of it took her breath away, so all she did was shake her head silently. 'Shall I fix it for you?'

Such anxiety to see her on her way hurt more than he

could possibly have realised, and Willow's heart was thudding heavily in despair, while threatening tears shimmered behind the lashes she kept carefully lowered. 'Thank you,' she whispered.

If only he had said one word to persuade her to stay, even if only for another day or two, she would have agreed without hesitation, whatever was in store for her. But instead he nodded his willingness to get her airline ticket for her, and she found it almost too much to bear suddenly. 'I'll drive you to the airport,' he promised. 'I guess you'd rather I took you than Richard.'

Willow nodded blindly and clung tightly to the balustrade, looking at the strong brown fingers that still enclosed hers. She was never going to see him again once she left Hawaii, and she wished she found it easier to face without feeling so completely wretched. 'That's—that's good of you, thank you.'

'Just leave everything to me,' Adam told her, and she nodded, then turned quickly and went on up the stairs before he realised how near she was to breaking down completely.

For about the hundredth time in just a few minutes, Willow glanced at the bedside clock, then put down the book she had been trying in vain to get interested in. She had done most of her packing, then soaked for a long time in a bath generously scented with her favourite bath essence, but she still found it hard to relax.

It was almost dark and the mingled scents of the garden were intensified as they always were at this time of day, so that everything was conducive to relaxation and sleep. Had she been dressed she would have walked for a while in the garden, but she had not long come from her bath and she sat curled up in the big armchair that stood by the window of her room, wearing only a thin pale green robe over a body that was still warm and moist and sweetly scented.

It would have taken very little to make her cry in earnest, although so far she had allowed only an odd tear to escape. Crying, she told herself wasn't going to solve anything, and if she appeared with red-rimmed eyes the next morning it was only going to give people the wrong impression. So for the moment she sat with her chin supported on one hand and propped on the arm of her chair, with a soft, misty look in her eyes as she contemplated a future without Adam.

It was a soft but insistent tapping on her door that roused her, and she stared at the door uncertainly for a moment. It was more than likely Madame le Brun, calling in on her way to bed to see if she was all right, and she brushed a hasty hand across her eyes before calling out 'Come in!'

'Willow?'

For a moment she stared in stunned surprise at Adam standing just inside the half-open door, then she scrambled swiftly to her feet, alarmingly reminded that the robe was very thin and that she had not yet put on her nightgown. His face was in shadow, for the light from the reading lamp by her chair was very limited, but it was sufficient for her to notice how his eyes moved slowly over her, boldly explicit yet oddly gentle too.

It reminded her that he had once seen her in even less than a thin robe, and a flush of warm colour flooded into her cheeks. The white shirt he wore gleamed in the shadows and threw his dark features and the strong column of his throat into deep relief, and Willow felt herself trembling as she tried to bring her emotions under control.

'I'm sorry,' said Adam, but making no attempt to leave. 'I didn't realise you were——' An expressive hand conveyed his meaning unmistakably and she drew the robe close to her throat. 'I saw your light on and thought you might still be up.'

'I—I am, as you see.' She was shivering as if she was cold, yet at the same time her body glowed with an inner warmth that seemed to emanate from the tall, lean masculine body that hovered in the doorway. 'I had a bath,' she explained unnecessarily, 'and I didn't bother to dress again, that's why I'm——'

'You look beautiful.'

The deep voice shivered along her spine and aroused all those disturbing emotions she had never been able to control. But she tried to resist the brief temptation she felt to close her eyes in sheer ecstasy, and so betray the effect it had. Snatching herself back to earth, she fluttered her hands vaguely.

'You—you'd better come right in,' she said, and barely resisted adding—someone might see you.

One dark brow remarked briefly on the invitation, but he did as she suggested and came right into the room, closing the door behind him carefully and quietly. As he came across the room towards her Willow's toes curled with sensual pleasure into the deep pile of the carpet, and her heart was racing wildly, making her hold her head at a curiously wary angle.

Adam eyed her steadily for a moment, then a smile showed just briefly in the shadowed greyness of his eyes. 'If you'd like to change your mind,' he suggested, 'I'll go. It isn't hard to understand why you're suspicious, you've had a pretty hard time lately.'

'I'm not suspicious.'

She spoke in a whisper, and with the soft glow of the lamp behind her she had a fragile and almost ethereal look that was enhanced by the flimsiness of the green robe. Yet there was nothing ethereal about the very feminine curves that the light material flattered and stressed, and Adam made no pretence of not noticing them.

'Most of what happened was partly my own fault,' she insisted huskily. 'I just didn't see Richard as he really is, even when you tried to warn me.'

Despite her efforts to prevent it, Adam caught and held her evasive eyes, and her heart had the urgency of a drumbeat, her whole body aching for the feel of his arms around her. 'You don't still want to marry him?' he asked, and Willow shook her head unhesitatingly.

'No, definitely not! I meant what I said earlier—I don't think I ever really wanted to marry him. It was just that we drifted into that—engagement, if you can call it that. He's good-looking and he can be incredibly charming when he likes—I don't know, it just—happened.'

'I know.' For a moment the grey eyes, dark as storm clouds, held hers steadily, then he nodded, as if he were finally convinced. He was much closer too, without her having noticed he had moved, and he reached out and lightly touched her cheek. 'Remember what I said?' he asked, and Willow gazed at him blankly. 'I said that if Richard didn't marry you, I would—remember?'

Her stomach felt a sudden awful chill and it was as if her heart had stopped beating altogether for a moment. Shaking her head slowly, she stared at him in horror. 'Oh no,' she whispered. 'Oh no, you haven't come here simply because of some—some——' She turned from him swiftly and stood with her hands on her arms, feeling shrunken suddenly. 'Go away,' she pleaded in a small flat voice. 'Please go away!'

'No, Willow, I'm not going away—and neither are you.'

He didn't move, nor did he say anything else, and eventually Willow felt obliged to turn and face him again, looking up at him through the concealing thickness of her lashes with eyes that looked as dark and hurt as a child's. Adam reached out and touched her face again, and there was nothing she could do to resist the need to rest her face in the broad warmth of his palm.

'Look at me!'

She did as he said, and saw the way his mouth was half-smiling. Her emotions were responding as they always did to him, however confused she was, and her body pulsed with the same wild abandonment that only Adam ever aroused in her, and she couldn't believe he had spoken of marrying her just because of some lighthearted remark he once made in jest!

'Adam!'

He had to know how she felt, how could he not? And

those light seductive fingers stroking over her cheeks moved slowly down to her neck. 'I couldn't be sure you really didn't want to marry Richard, or if you were just putting on a show of British stiff upper lip,' he told her in a voice that was far more seductive than the words he used. 'Grand'mère advised me to stay away from you until morning when she hoped you'd be feeling a little less— shattered, but I had to speak with you.'

That look of desire was in his eyes again, dispelling any reservations she might have had left, and she was suddenly sure—too sure to doubt her own feelings or Adam's as she looked up into his face with its stormy grey eyes, and half- smiled. 'Then speak with me,' she invited in a shivery little whisper, and Adam's hands slid down to the small of her back, pressing her close to him.

Through the flimsy robe her body responded to the pressure of hard fingers, and the broad flat palms of his hands burned into her flesh, bringing her closer still to the unyielding virility of him. Lifting her arms Willow put them around his neck, heedless of the fact that the robe gaped open and the soft swell of her breasts flinched briefly from the vee of flesh his shirt exposed.

She had seen that dark, raw look of desire before, but she had never before felt so completely uninhibited about responding to it, and his mouth hovered only briefly above hers before plunging downward and taking it with a sensuous fierceness that stopped her breath.

What seemed like an eternity later he lifted his head and looked down into her eyes, his own gleaming like wet granite. 'You won't go?' he whispered, and the warmth of his words fluttered against her lips. 'You won't leave me, will you, Willow? You don't know how I need you—stay with me!'

For a moment it seemed he might be offering the same kind of arrangement Richard had wanted, but she realised that she would stay with Adam, whatever the terms. 'On the same terms that Richard wanted?' she suggested, and held her breath while he studied her for a moment.

'Would you come to me on those terms?' he challenged, and Willow looked at him for a long time with her big shining eyes.

'Yes,' she admitted. 'Yes, I would.'

'You little wanton, I believe you would!'

He bound her close again and his strong hands caressed her nakedness through the thin robe, pushing the silky material down from her shoulders and burying his mouth in the smooth, scented softness of her skin. Sliding her arms around him, Willow pressed her fingers into the broad muscular back and thrilled to the force that aroused every nerve in her body to respond. And when he took her mouth once again she moaned softly in her fierce need for him.

'I mean to have you,' Adam whispered hoarsely against her mouth. '*And* I'm going to marry you, just as I said I would.' She looked up at him with her eyes shining and her lips parted, tingling and eager to be kissed again. 'When I made that promise I never dreamed I'd have the chance to keep it,' he went on, and kissed her with an almost savage determination. 'I wanted you from the moment Richard brought you here and I prayed he wouldn't change course and marry you after all, because if he had I think I'd have gone out of my mind!'

'Would you?'

Her eyes teased him very gently, and he pulled her closer again, his eyes gleaming with that irresistible desire she could never deny, and his hands pressed hard into her bare shoulders. 'Don't tease, my sweetheart,' he warned her darkly. 'I'm asking you to marry me.'

His breath warmed her mouth and the hard urgency of his body aroused all those wild and irresistible desires she could never learn to control. Laying her hands on the brown column of his throat, she stroked gently as she smiled up at him. 'Will I have to go in fear of Marsha Sai-Hung for the rest of my life if I do?' she whispered, and he slid the silky robe still farther down her arms.

'You go in fear of no one,' Adam promised. 'Marsha knows when she's licked. If she ever did stand a chance, my love, she lost it the moment I saw you standing sweet mother-naked in that mountain pool. I'd never seen anything so perfect and so desirable, and I vowed then that I'd take you from Richard if I could.'

The colour in her cheeks burned hotly when she remembered, and she looked up at him reproachfully. 'How could you remind me of that!'

'How could I not be reminded every time I see you?' Adam demanded in a deep and shiveringly seductive voice. His arms tightened around her and he looked down at her with gleaming eyes. 'Now give me an answer, damn you—will you marry me?'

Pressing still closer, Willow smiled. 'I'll marry you, my darling,' she promised. 'I love you.'

'I love you.' The words were like an echo of her own, and his mouth sought hers again with a fierce hungry urgency. When he eventually raised his head again he looked at her for a long moment, then shook his head. 'You're too much of a temptation,' he murmured. 'It's as well grand'mère is here to chaperone you.' He bent and kissed her bare shoulder, his mouth warm and lingering. 'And we'll stick to that date she's arranged too, because I'm not going to wait for you until the whole shebang has been organised over again!'

With her mouth close to his ear Willow smiled mischievously to herself. 'Did you know that she asked me to marry you instead of Richard, quite some time ago?' she asked, and when Adam looked down at her again it was clear that he did know.

'And you turned it down,' he accused.

Laughing, Willow shook her head. 'Only because I thought you wouldn't like what she had in mind for you,' she told him, and Adam kissed her hard.

'Little idiot!' he said.

'Adam——'

His mouth was buried deeply in hers once more, and in the wild abandoned moments that followed she thought no more of going home. She thought no more about anything.

Harlequin® Plus

A WORD ABOUT THE AUTHOR

When British-born and -bred Rebecca Stratton left school, she began a series of jobs that included everything—from punch-card operator to machinist in a suspender factory! But for her, there was only one real goal: someday she was going to be a professional writer.

And at long last, when she was forty-five, she left a safe and secure job to devote all her time to writing. Her first book, a romantic novel, was sent off to a publisher, and while waiting for a reply she completed two more manuscripts. Then came the joyous news: her first novel, *The Golden Madonna* (Romance #1748) had been accepted. She was on her way!

For Rebecca Stratton, a writing career means interviews by the local papers and speaking engagements before local clubs. But most of all, and best of all, it means settling down to the real nitty-gritty: plain hard work.

The bestselling epic saga of the Irish
An intriguing and passionate story that spans 400 years.

FIRST...
The Defiant

Lady Elizabeth Hatton, highborn
Englishwoman, was not above using
her position to get what she wanted
...and more than anything in the
world she wanted Rory
O'Donnell, the fiery Irish rebel.
But it was an alliance that promised
only ruin....

THEN...
The Survivors

Against a turbulent background of
political intrigue and royal
corruption, the determined,
passionate Shanna O'Hara searched
for peace in her beloved
but troubled Ireland. Meanwhile
in England, hot-tempered
Brenna Coke fought against
a loveless marriage....

THE O'HARA DYNASTY by MARY CANON

'High adventure with steamy passion."
—*Glamour*

'Impressive, compelling...the sweep of a saga."
—*Good Housekeeping*

'An epic saga that should please...those who enjoy
a rich novel."

—Patricia Matthews
author of *Tides of Love*

AND NOW...
The Renegades

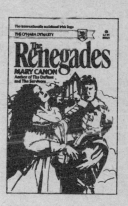

Under the tyranny of Cromwell's
Puritan rule, the Irish fought vainly
for their freedom. Caught in the
struggle, Maggie O'Hara waged her
own fierce war against marriage to a
ruthless Englishman. And
thousands of miles away, on the
slave plantations of Barbados,
another battle was being waged—
that of a handsome Irish rebel
determined to flee bondage and
claim the woman he loved.

Each volume contains more than 500 pages of superb
reading for only $2.95.

Available wherever paperback books are sold or through

WORLDWIDE READER SERVICE

IN THE U.S.
P.O. Box 22188
Tempe, AZ 85282

IN CANADA
649 Ontario Street
Stratford, Ontario N5A 6W2

Readers rave about Harlequin romance fiction...

"I absolutely adore Harlequin romances! They are fun and relaxing to read, and each book provides a wonderful escape."
—N.E.,* Pacific Palisades, California

"Harlequin is the best in romantic reading."
—K.G., Philadelphia, Pennsylvania

"Harlequin romances give me a whole new outlook on life."
—S.P., Mecosta, Michigan

"My praise for the warmth and adventure your books bring into my life."
—D.F., Hicksville, New York

*Names available on request.